AF411117

Corona of Thorns?

or

Corona of Life?

Changing Church in the Covid Context

Corona of Thorns?

or

Corona of Life?

Changing Church in the Covid Context

Editors

Francis Gonsalves & Vinod Victor

2020

Corona of Thorns? or Corona of Life? Changing Church in the Covid Context— Published by the Indian Society for Promoting Christian Knowledge (ISPCK), Post Box 1585, Kashmere Gate, Delhi-110006.

© ISPCK, 2020

All rights reserved. No part of this book may be reproduced or transmitted in any form or by any means, electronic, mechanical, photocopying, recording, or by any information storage and retrieval system, without the prior permission in writing from the publisher.

The views expressed in the book are those of the contributors and the publisher takes no responsibility for any of the statements.

Online order: http://ispck.org.in/book.php

Also available on amazon.in

ISBN: 978-81-946569-1-3

eBook ISBN: 978-81-946569-2-0

Laser typeset by

ISPCK, Post Box 1585, 1654, Madarsa Road, Kashmere Gate, Delhi-110006
• *Tel:* 23866323

e-mail: ashish@ispck.org.in • ella@ispck.org.in
website: www.ispck.org.in

Contents

Foreword

*"For his anger is but for a moment;
his favour is for a lifetime. Weeping may linger for the night,
but joy comes with the morning"* (Psalm 30:5)

This book '*Corona of Thorns? or Corona of Life? Changing Church in the Covid Context*' is not just another publication, rather, it promises to be a life changing book. On the one hand, it raises questions that have emerged in our minds and hearts all through the time we were under lockdowns, and, on the other, it attempts to provide some answers, too. Many committed Indian Christians collectively express in the book what you can expect of Church and Society after this crisis.

I know from my own experience the multiple questions that I had in my mind. Indeed, all of us—and not just those practising the Christian faith—had many questions in mind. Every day was a challenge during the peak of the pandemic, and the situation continues to be worrisome beyond the lockdowns. As we read this book, we will remember many persons who have had unique experiences and many unforgettable events that have shaped us in ways known and unknown.

Many were lonely, sad and depressed. Others were optimistic and enjoyed quality time with their family. Formerly, on any regular day, many families would not have the time to have a meal together or even pray together. But the Lord has made all this possible. Those who were not going to church went online for Sunday worship. Perhaps this gave us a time to review our relationships not only with those who we live with, but also with those who are distant. Perhaps we phoned and spoke to those we had not even thought of as we ran the 'rat race'. Our focus had shifted to material things of the world.

No matter what happens to us and our world, the evil forces can never stop the work of our Lord. What God has designed for us will be done. It is for us to pray: "Thy will be done on earth as it is in heaven." God wants us to return to Him and to be united to Him.

We often sing this song:

> Trust in the Lord and don't despair,
> He is a friend so true!
> No matter what your troubles are,
> Jesus will see you through.
> Sing, when the day is bright;
> Sing, through the darkest night
> Every day, all the way,
> Let us sing, sing, sing!

We need to sing songs of thanksgiving despite trials and troubles, especially in times like these when there is isolation and uncertainty. Truly, we have hope in the Almighty who will never let us down. This battle is not over yet (Mt 24:7). But let us in one spirit pray that the Lord will heal this world and his healing power will flow all through the world.

The Most Rt. Rev. Dr P.C. Singh

Moderator, The Church of North India Synod

Bishop of Jabalpur

President, ISPCK

Preface

Corona of Thorns? or Corona of Life?

Changing Church in the Covid Context

Every catastrophe opens up windows of opportunity. While there's no disputing the fact that Covid-19 has had a devastating impact on life the world over, it's also true that it has provided a pleroma of possibilities for the world to be a better place if only we make the most of this *Kairos*. 'Corona' stems from the Latin root, meaning, a crown or a wreath. Used to name a virus as early as 1930 and seen in print from 1968 it has perhaps become the most widely used word ever since the December 2019 strain of the virus hit headlines worldwide. In each and every sphere of life Covid is redefining the way we comprehend reality. The Church is no exception.

The Christian symbol of the crown is synonymous with the 'crown of thorns' that was thrust upon Jesus during his passion (Mt 27:29; Mk 15:17; Jn 19:2,5). It was part of the suffering that made salvation possible. Though intended to inflict more pain and add insult to injury, it slowly got transformed into a sign of hope—that 'Crown of Life' (Jam 1:12; Rev 2:10)—which was a powerful element of the eschatological promise. The two juxtaposed offer a glimpse of the pain that global citizens are undergoing and also the pregnant possibilities that are emerging.

'*Corona of Thorns?*' or '*Corona of Life?*' in the title raises questions. We are all raising questions, facing questions, evading questions, answering questions. For the first time in our lifetime, perhaps, we do not have answers. Or, the answers we tentatively give are not backed by that certainty that scientists, doctors, politicians, pundits, theologians, pastors and teachers once presumed to have. So, we remain silent with these questions and surrender to God, even as we attempt to envision a '*Changing Church in the Covid Context*', which is the subtitle of this book, containing articles by committed Indian Christians from different backgrounds and with diverse viewpoints.

This book is divided into two broad sections. The first entitled '*Today's Corona of Thorns?*' has articles that raise questions: Should we return to the 'normal'? Is it not an abnormal that we were celebrating as normal? There are articles of personal experiences of reaching out to the needy and of analysing how Covid has adversely affected the poor, the vulnerable, migrants, daily wage workers, women and children. We are reminded of our collective responsibility, our guilt, and the debt we owe to those who have suffered, sacrificed and died. We are made aware of how 'poor-unfriendly and excluding' our world and its health care systems are, and how the Church perhaps needs deconstruction and reconstruction to remake it as the Body of Christ in our world, today. The thrust of this section is largely contextual, self-critical, but with a view to usher in much-needed renewal and church reform.

The second section entitled '*Tomorrow's Corona of Life?*' envisions future Church and Christian life and mission from the perspective of various groups: youth, women and families. The closing down of places of worship to contain the pandemic has redefined the way that these groups understand Church. The lockdowns have made everyone enter deep within to realise how interconnected and interdependent we are with each other and with mother earth. The articles in this section also discuss the possibilities of an e-Church, of online worship, of common prayers with believers of other religions, of marrying science and religion, and of bolder initiatives in the realms of economics, ecumenism and ecology. Indeed, no longer can the Church think in parochial terms and make the *paroika*, the parish its' world; for now, the world has become one parish.

Just as the 'corona of thorns' and the 'corona of life' are two sides of the same coin, so are the two sections of the book interwoven—with the contributors realistic about the seriousness of the pandemic, yet never losing faith in the God of Life. This God of the exodus, of the jubilee, and of the covenant in Christ, who embraces all peoples and mother earth, is the steady anchor, the Great I AM, of our changing Church in the Covid context.

The authors see the need of moving from a mere charity mode to the justice mode that will ensure a better world for everyone, especially the 'least' of Christ's sisters and brothers. Although the authors present viewpoints that differ from each other, all of them agree: 'All are not safe until everyone is safe'. Covid is both a pandemic and a portal. It is for us to mitigate the pain and grab the opportunities offered. The book offers a bird's eye view on how that can be done meaningfully.

The Editors

Introduction

We began the New Year 2020 prayerfully, with great hope and deep trust in God. Everything seemed to be going on well for a while. However, we soon began getting news about a deadly virus, corona, that was creating havoc in China …. We still hoped and prayed, thinking that this tragedy would not affect us. It was not to be …..

From China, Covid-19 soon began making its way all around the world. It travelled to Italy, then Spain and many other European countries. It then crossed over to the USA and made its lethal presence felt in India, too. In its journey, Covid-19 has left a trail of darkness, disease and death. It has created fear and a phobia that has deeply affected the hearts and minds of people, worldwide. Thousands of its victims are still struggling to fight it or have lost their lives.

Covid-19 has not spared anyone. The world's richest and technologically advanced nations have suffered as much as the poorest countries. Everyone seemed helpless. The whole world seemed crushed as lockdown after lockdown was imposed leading to economies collapsing and human beings becoming jobless and hopeless.

In the midst of Corona's darkness and death, there are many heroes: doctors, nurses, paramedical staff, police personnel, emergency services, social activists, counsellors, government officials and some political leaders. These brave hearts have fought against Covid-19 and continue to do so. They were forced to take tough decisions, some of which were painful.

There have been great changes in the religious realm as well. Religious places were locked down and there were prohibitions to assemble for religious ceremonies. Many believers also began questioning the presence of God, the role of religion, the meaning of life and the relevance of rituals. This book attempts to highlight issues which people are facing. It will help us to understand Covid-19 and its impact positively and constructively.

I thank all the writers for their contributions in this book. I congratulate you all and pray that this book will bring manifold positive blessings and rebuild humanity in every possible way.

God bless you!

Rt. Rev. Silvans S. Christian
Chairperson, ISPCK
Bishop of Gujarat, CNI Gujarat Diocese

I

TODAY'S CORONA OF THORNS?

1

Covid-19 and the Vulnerable

Vincent Rajkumar

Looking at the Lockdown from the Perspective of the Poor

It's anyone's guess how seriously Covid-19 will impact India. The complete lack of preparation that has defined government responses is accompanied by a conspicuous lack of preparedness and testing. As a result, in the fraction of a second, more than eighty million migrant workers and daily wage employees became jobless and homeless and lost their livelihood. This utter lack of foresight and preparedness forced the Prime Minister to perform a series of largely rhetorical gestures, with sudden, rapidly announced lockdown of the entire country on March 24—at just four hours' prior notice, with no real warning or preparation, let alone any carefully thought-out plan for millions of migrant workers and their families.

As a consequence of this unseen and unprepared lockdown, millions of poor people have been robbed of their jobs and income, and been deprived of their livelihoods, imposing a disproportionate burden on the poor and those who survive just above the poverty line. This state of affairs has intersected with their pre-existing disadvantages, bringing to the fore inequalities, discrimination and anxieties. When it comes to the urban migrant workers, the difficulties due to the lockdown have begun to intersect with their existing vulnerabilities.

In India eighty millions of the workforce is made up of the self-employed, casual labour on daily wages, and informal workers without any social protection. The most vulnerable people in this sector are the migrant workers: the construction workers, painters, delivery boys, cooks, cleaners and factory workers, among others, who have travelled far to eke out a meagre livelihood, almost always without social protection, healthcare benefits and a minimum, decent standard of living. Although the lockdown is an inevitable solution to control the pandemic, its implementation was abrupt, poorly conceived and underprepared. A prior planned strategy of dealing with urban migrants, employees in the informal sector, and livelihood options for daily wage earners, migrant workers, and students was completely missing.

The sudden lockdown not only exposed millions of migrant workers and students to the virus while travelling by air, rail or local transport and some even walking barefoot back to their homes hundreds of kilometres away, but it also pushed an unprecedented number of people at risk who were travelling with them and their family members, particularly elderly in their homes. Considering the time lag between the first case reported in India and the countrywide lockdown, the preparation could have been much better. Besides, the country failed to prevent the import of the virus and break the channels to contain the spread with an early shutdown of international travel and closing of country borders.

Misery of Migrants Unwelcome at Home

This pandemic-led lockdown and crisis have not only pulled down the plagued health care system but also shows the lacunae in building preparedness to counter the pandemic. For migrant workers, the trade-off between getting sick and going hungry was no choice. These migrants were left with no choice but to head towards their hometowns. With public transport stopped, many walked mind-boggling distances and the rest remain stranded on the way. The migrants who are currently travelling on the roads are burdening the health systems and also impacting their own health. It is so unfortunate that the migrant workers who have made it to their villages have often found they are no longer welcomed. In several villages the local villagers put up barricades at the entry points and hung posters, warning the migrants against entering the village before a health check-up.

With no basic and almost non-existent public health facilities, testing centres, infrastructure or trained staff in the villages, our health system is rendered useless when it is needed the most because the current model of healthcare system is largely built up of private health care facilities as social welfare schemes and medical insurance will not work in our rural areas. It is clear that what was done as a public health measure to protect people from the Covid-19 threat has snowballed into a major economic crisis for the urban poor in general and migrant labourers in particular.

In the recent past, there were debates over the nature of India's rural society—on whether it was intrinsically good or bad. These debates are no longer relevant. The village is, however, still relevant, at least for the vast number of urban workers. But in the policies of the government we experience a problem that it does not acknowledge the right of villages to flourish as human habitations with their own distinctive future. But they deserve to have new sites and forms of livelihood. They also deserve systems of health and education that are not designed as feeders to distant centres. Initiatives in this direction will make both cities and villages more sustainable and capable of coping with the kind of crisis we are currently facing.

For this to happen, we need a more humane government responsive to the basic needs of its people, especially the poor. But the present government's lack of sympathy and concern for the stranded migrant workers clearly shows that the system doesn't work for everyone. Most shocking is the slew of controversial reforms announced by the government in the last episode of five-part serial on the government's stimulus package which was nothing but a loan-mela and that too for the rich and the industrial barons. Instead of addressing the migrant worker crisis, the government has embarked on greater privatisation and further opening up of the economy to foreign capital. It has thrown open coal, defence production, space travel, among other areas, to the private sector. These contentious pieces of economic reforms wouldn't be counted as rescue packages anywhere.

Over and above the economic fallout on poor sections of society, it is wrong and unethical to enforce a lockdown without any consideration to the plight of the poor. Instead, the government used this opportunity of crisis to initiate a new move to bring certain changes in the labour laws and to privatise several of the public undertakings that will not give any hope to the migrants who are in distress. The government's lack of sympathy and concern for the stranded migrant workers clearly shows that the system doesn't work for everyone. No wonder, migrant labourers across India have told reporters that they won't return to see such humiliation again. No one is surprised at their courage and determination to return to their homes mocking the government's schemes and promises.

An effective response in India at this juncture must consider not only the behaviour of the pathogen but also the socio-economic and cultural characteristics of the pandemic. Many experts have adequately articulated that homelessness during the time of quarantine, loss of livelihoods, lack of health care, job loss, financial insecurity and hunger can make the lives of a large number of people more miserable. This would mean that India needs to take better care of its urban migrants, most of who seem to have lost their jobs, shelter and food. Furthermore, India will have to care for the rural landless and small or marginal farmers who are finding it difficult to harvest or sell their produce due to the lockdown. This is the kairos time for India to foresee the impacts of the pandemic on social, economic and health fronts and take adequate steps to minimise the damage during the ongoing pandemic and to be resilient to face any future pandemics.

Conclusion: Challenge for Collective Action beyond Mere Charity

Covid-19 is much more than a health crisis. Already we are beginning to understand the potential socio-economic impact of this pandemic. In this changing scenario, with unique challenges that threaten the health and well-being of the population, it is imperative that the government and the community at large collectively rise to the occasion and face these challenges simultaneously, inclusively and sustainably. Social determinants of health and economic issues must be dealt with a consensus on ethical principles: universalism, justice, dignity, security and human rights.

In a country like India where nearly eighty per cent of economic activity comes from the informal sector, small temporary handouts of cash and rations are simply not enough. In the long-run, a greater investment into clinical, biomedical, micro-biological and public health research for detecting the threat in advance, building resilient socio-economic and health systems, developing affordable diagnosis and understanding in advance the socio-economic, demographic and gendered impacts are of foremost importance. This approach will be of valuable service to humanity in realising the dream of the right to life and livelihood.

2

No Return to the Normal: Church after Covid-19

Felix Wilfred

Pandemic is not anything new to humanity. The ten plagues of Egypt are well-known. We do not know how many people it killed. But we do know that the Black Death of 1324 decimated around 200 million people when the world population was just about 475 million. The outbreak of this plague shook Europe and caused social, political, economic and cultural upheavals of an unprecedented magnitude. The Spanish Flu of the early twentieth century killed 100 million, and there have been other smaller pandemics of lesser proportions. Millions throughout history fell victim to the recurrent outbreak of smallpox in India, and people flocked to the goddess of smallpox – *Mariamma* or *Śītalādevī* – who both causes the epidemic and cures the same.

None of the epidemics in history ripped open the persistent inequality and callous injustice of our world to the extent Covid-19 has done. This epidemic is the symptom of an unjust world whose heavy tilt of balance forebodes calamity of apocalyptic proportions. The pandemic requires a moral response on the part of the Church. It calls for a rethinking on the priorities of the Church, and a thorough reform of its life, worship, and mission. Instead of speaking in general terms, here I would like to reflect more specifically on the Indian Roman Catholic Church, which I know a little better than the other Churches.

I could hear the groanings and deep sighs of many faithful for whom anything is bearable except the dreadful plight of not being able to go to the church. They yearn to participate in the Eucharist and are longing to go on pilgrimage to their favourite Marian shrines, miraculous shrines of Saint Antony, Saint Sebastian, and Infant Jesus, attend novenas devoutly, participate in eucharistic processions, reciting the rosary, and singing those mellifluous familiar hymns …..The nostalgia is too painful. The routine that had become normal is being sorely missed. Catholics who moved in this religious land of promise, now suddenly feel exiled. Like the Jews in exile on the banks of River Babylon, Catholics long to go back to the familiar religious world. Hence, the frantic question: "When are they opening the churches?".

Numerous bishops and priests who have been pontificating, all of a sudden, became clueless in the situation of lockdown. Their voices fell silent. I wonder what they have been doing, completely cut off from the constituency of the faithful assembled in the churches. Once the familiar world ebbed out, they have become like fish out of water. They seem to be eagerly waiting to return to the 'normal'. The sad thing is that there cannot be any return to the normal. For, the normal was the problem. We need to think of the post Covid-19 situation in new terms rather than merely restoring the familiar religious world. The experience of the macabre pandemic is an occasion to rethink our worship, faith, and our mission from a different level and perspective.

The Catholic Church, which has been obsessed with the externalities of sacraments, needs to now focus on what Jesus advocated, "worship in spirit and truth" (Jn 4:23-24). We have identified the divine with a particular locality and worship with certain forms of rituals. We have locked Jesus in the tabernacle. The clerics are securely in possession of the key to Jesus – so it would appear. It is a metaphor of what is happening in the Church. Without the sacraments performed by the clergy, the way is barred to Jesus, to the divine mystery. No wonder that the faithful find themselves religiously devastated.

The response of Jesus to the Samaritan woman reflects what kind of worship Jesus had in mind. Spirit can never be imprisoned in places and objects. It is always on the move and does not get stuck anywhere, neither in the temple of Jerusalem nor in our churches and sacraments. As an early Christian writer, Dionysius Areopagite put it, "God's centre is everywhere; God's circumference is nowhere." Limiting God to any one place or object is a sacrilegious distortion of the divine, a fashioning of God according to our image and needs. To be able to worship God in truth, we need to be first of all seekers of truth. The truth is a power that gives freedom, and there is no limit. It can come from any quarter. Truth is an ever-receding horizon, which keeps us moving in the right direction. This quest keeps us changing and transforming ourselves all the while. The sincere search for truth, and abiding by it is the best worship we could do.

There has been a colossal failure in the Indian Church in deepening the faith of the people and in helping them worship in spirit and in truth. Had these taken place, they would not feel so lost and helpless as they do now. They would know that their faith and their worship will continue even without the crutches of churches and sacraments. These are not an end in themselves but a means to something beyond. A deep faith anchored in divine mystery will worship it first and foremost in the heart. It will worship God, gazing at the splendour of creation.

Yes, nature is the first book God wrote even before the Bible. The scriptures help us find God in the wonderful creation, in the universe. Astronomers tell us that there are more stars in the universe than all the grains of sand on earth. It would be necessary in the post Covid-19 Catholic Church to foster a different faith-formation that will help people find God and commune with the divine mystery anywhere and under any circumstance. Then, the whole world is a sacrament of God. All of life can be turned into worship. There is need to assist people to read their own lives and help them encounter and worship God. As a concerned pastor, Paul encourages the believers of his community in Rome to precisely turn their life into worship: "I appeal to you therefore, brethren, by the mercies of God, to present your bodies as a living sacrifice, holy and acceptable to God, which is your spiritual worship.… Be transformed by the renewal of your mind, that you may prove what is the will of God, what is good and acceptable and perfect" (Rom 12:1-2).

To be able to discover God everywhere and worship the divine, we need an adult faith. By adult faith, I do not mean a faith professed only with the head, with human reason. No, faith needs to get embodied in the materiality of everyday life. Adult faith is different from the 'faith' in which we enter into a commercial relationship with God (*do ut des*): we offer sacrifice, undertake fasting, go on pilgrimage, circumambulate churches, perform religious activities to obtain favours from God. The traditional Catholic sacramental and devotional life mostly consisted of certain sets of practices. Adult faith is one in which there is total trust and abandonment to God, as Abraham did when he undertook an unknown journey and when Job suffered with unshaken faith.

The Psalms are a beautiful example of worship, praise and thanks to God with adult faith throughout the vicissitudes of life—nagging fears, anxieties, failures, painful losses, but also the joy of life, contentment, experiences of love, friendship and solidarity. "Clap your hands, all peoples! Shout to God with loud songs of joy!" (Ps 47:1). Every Christian can express her faith and worship God as the psalmists did, incorporating worship with life. It does not require any church-building or particular location or sacramental performance by the clergy. The post Covid Church we imagine will be one that will not limit the encounter with God to sacraments and the clerical mediation of it. The pandemic has exposed how the horizon of our faith and worship had shrunk, without our realizing it. We now need a new opening.

When Jesus returned to the Father, I imagine, he showed the Father his five wounds as the proof of his life on earth. Those scars were the cost of his identification with suffering humanity. The exit from Covid-19 should signify a turning point for the Church. How could the Church go to the normal, and be the same, after having witnessed the crucifixion of so many innocent people, the most horrendous and heartrending stories of the marginalized and powerless migrant workers? These are the unsung heroes and heroines who built the country with their toil, sweat and blood, and now have become throwaway objects and fearsome carriers of the virus to be shunned away. Without jobs, without any means of survival, millions are exposed to death, not of coronavirus, but of hunger. The walking of migrant children miles and miles barefoot in blazing heat on the melting roads with no food, with no security; the collapsing of a young man on the ground out of sheer exhaustion, are potent reminders of the way of the cross and the crucifixion. A fifteen-year-old young girl, Jyoti Kumari, peddling a cycle 1,200 kilometres from Gurugram to Bihar, carrying her ailing father to reach home is a story of courage, hope and resurrection. If the Church indeed participates in this story of the passion and resurrection—this pascal liturgy on the streets of the country—it will not be anymore the same.

When the survival and safety of over forty-five million migrant labourers were hanging in balance, where was the leadership of the Catholic Church in India? What did they say about this inhumanity heaped on those who gave their labour for the country and were betrayed and stranded with nowhere to go? What sense of humanity and justice did this leadership show towards millions of daily labourers who were left in the lurch to feed their hungry children? I think the Indian Catholic Church has a lot to introspect seriously about how it has faced a humanitarian crisis caused by the pandemic in the nation. We were told by the Indian Catholic leadership to peal the bells in the churches on 22 March, and probably also to bang pots and pans. We were told to say *Namaste* and not shake hands; report to the doctor when there are symptoms; refrain from kissing the cross; to keep the holy water scoop dry in the Church—the kind of stereotype advisory we hear day in and day out from every Tom, Dick and Harry on television screens, radio, what's app and so on. What substantial message did the Catholic Church leadership deliver to the faithful, except liturgical minutiae? Did the Catholic Church have any message for the people of the nation at a highly critical time? How true it is that the dearth of leadership goes along with dearth of vision and imagination. Moreover, the Indian Catholic Church leadership seems to be elitist and has an upper middle-class mindset. It is eager to protect itself rather than stand by the poor, who receive but lip-service.

The Indian Catholic Church will need to rethink its life and worship, mission and leadership in new terms. It will have its ears on the rough road of reality to hear the foot-tapping of the migrants on the way, which should continuously prick its conscience when it is tempted to exhibit its power with massive churches and institutions, or act pompously as we witness in the religious choreography and unending jubilee celebrations of all imaginable kinds. The Covid-19 should serve as a period of purification—*metanoia*—of the Catholic Church from cankerous clericalism, the desert of careerism, ostentatious triumphalism, insipid liturgical routinization, theatric religious performances, endemic strife over power and property, and clandestine sexual misadventures of clerics.

After having experienced Covid-19, how could the Indian Catholic Church return to the normal? No, it needs to come out of the pandemic, repentant and converted and with a new mindset: *novus habitus mentis*. It should have learnt some hard lessons. We cannot sell justice for thirty pieces of silver—for the blessings from the presiding deities of power. The renewed Church will be committed resolutely to driving out the virus of injustice embedded lethally in our regnant political, social, economic, and cultural systems. This Church will alleviate the suffering of the poor, and wipe away the tears of the innocent victims. The virus of injustice, unfortunately, cannot be driven out by banging pots and pans from housetops. It requires that the Church comes down to the dusty soil, to get sullied and dirty – as Pope Francis would say – for having been on the street to stand in solidarity with the poor, the powerless, the migrants, the marginalized and the victims. Could we hope for a different Catholic Church in post Covid-19 India?

3

Fear Not for I Am with You

Rini Ralte

Snapshots of a Lockdown and Resultant Knockdown

A lockdown is usually announced to help people tide over difficult times. However, Prime Minister Narendra Modi's notice of a lockdown on the night of March 23, which came into force on March 24, was calamitous. It gave people only four hours to collect provisions and meet other essential needs. This resulted in a chaotic situation for most people, especially the poor. In this article, I shall share some of my experiences mainly of the migrant workers from the Northeast states who were stranded because of the lockdown.

Within a day of the imposition of the lockdown, it became clear that not everyone was suffering in the same way and to same extent. Except for minor difficulties, the lockdown was not really affecting rich individuals and wealthy families. There were difficulties, for instance, in buying masks and sanitizers which were just not available or were too expensive. But, worse still, cries of anxiety and fear were soon heard. These were cries for survival; for, many found themselves without a job, without wages for the work they had done, without a home since they could not pay the rent immediately, and without even food. This was a moment of intense worry and fear.

There are many sad and shocking incidents that I witnessed. There were four lockdowns from March 24 to May 31. The effects of each of these were disastrous for thousands of people. At the first one, many workers were not paid their wages and salaries for the month of March. While thousands began walking back to their villages, others stayed locked up in their small shelters, almost starving. People began to eat picked up mangoes fallen from trees as their food when nothing else was available. Families of five members would survive on half a kilogram of dal and a cup of tea for breakfast. There were cases of breastfeeding mothers' milk running out for not having proper food for months.

Added to the difficulties in food and shelter were the struggles to stay safe and uninfected by the corona virus. When people are struggling to buy, cook and eat sufficient food, how can they think about and afford masks and sanitizers? The much-needed social distancing, too, becomes impossible for the poor huddled together with nowhere to go. The 'stay home' can be comfortable for those working from home on cellphones and laptops. But, for others with no job security and no money in hand, life became unbearable.

Online with the Northeast Helpline: Personal Experiences
I am part of the Northeast Solidarity team in Bangalore. The Northeast Helpline number was ringing constantly, sometimes, fifty to seventy times a day; other times even

hundred calls were received. Most of the callers expressed their dire need for food and also financial help to pay their house rent. The anxiety and the fear of survival levels were very high. We started our campaign with a slogan, 'Hunger is real, please donate!' We shared the urgent needs of stranded people, which resulted in some NGOs and many individuals contributing the provisions.

The volunteer team of Northeast Solidarity was formed within four days of the lockdown to distribute food in Bangalore. The volunteers were courageous in risking their own lives while serving others since they are family folks— mothers, fathers, sisters and brothers—who are vulnerable, too. While giving messages like 'stay safe' and 'stay home' they themselves had to venture out; for if they didn't, who would distribute food to the starving people? The volunteers were truly doing a difficult task having only one option: either stay home or stay out to deliver food. All the volunteers said, "We will deliver food and God is there to protect us, we commit our lives to God and God will take care of us."

Being a volunteer in the team that collected and distributed food to the hungry people—for the entire period of sixty-six days of the lockdowns from March 27 to May 31—was for me a source of deep happiness and satisfaction. I often prayed very hard to God to protect me and my family and the word of God came to me again and again: *"I will be with you"*. This feeling of being accompanied and protected by God was so empowering and real.

My experience of food distribution is so empowering and unforgettable. Initially, when I began getting calls on the helpline, I really did not know how to proceed. For instance, a retired military officer called and offered to make food packets which we distributed. During the sixty-six days we regularly received ration packs and kept on distributing to those most in need. The total distribution reached to over fifty thousand kilograms of rice and other food items like dal, oil, sugar, salt, vegetables, potatoes, onions, toothpaste and soap. We reached out to five thousand two hundred and fifty families. Our storage rooms always seemed full and we hardly knew from where people were donating so generously. In all this, I experienced that constant assurance: *"Fear not, I am with you."*

Conclusion: Kairos Moment of the Life-Giving God

The days of Covid-19 have been dark with sad news from all over. Of course, even in the Northeast communities, the worst affected are women and children. On the one hand, we are all burdened by our fears and worries; yet, on the other hand, there is joy in reaching out to others needier than ourselves. It is my joy to live a life beyond fear; it is a new inspiration that the word of God is relevant in our own times. It is a *Kairos* moment when God has a new name 'a life giver' and comes to us as ration-provider, ration-distributor and counselor to help those in fear.

We are not sure how long the after effects of the Covid-19 pandemic will last. All we are sure about is a new theology as people loved and cared for by God. God confronts situations of fear, starvation and anxiety. It is for us to remember those words said to Prophet Isaiah (41:10):

> Fear not, for I *am* with you;
> Be not dismayed, for I *am* your God.
> I will strengthen you,
> Yes, I will help you,

This "*fear not for I am with you!*" is a new affirmation of faith and action.

4

Deconstructing Church, Building Christ-Communities:
Opportunity of a Fleeting Covid Moment

Asir Ebenezer

'Learning to be *Ekklesia*' was the theme of the first ever webinar offered by the National Council of Churches in India (NCCI) in the context of the corona virus holding sway over all the earth, nay, peoples of the earth—all at once and everywhere. This was an offering in a post-Easter context when the disciples sought to see Jesus inside a closed and sealed context in which his lifeless body had been kept whilst he was already amidst his own, as he had said, by the Galilean Sea inviting the disciples to come over and comprehend the life that transcends death and gets transformed in living-out faith.

Christians were shut out of their four-walled and closeted contexts where they went to meet God; lived out their faith in multifarious ways and then came back to the supposedly mundane. Was it a heritage inherited from going up to the

Temple? Or, was it a legacy of going out to the Tent outside the camp? Was it a division of the sacred and the sacrilegious that is perpetuated through exclusivist prejudices of the times such as the casteist divisions and that of pure and impure? Whatever it may be, it stands in stark contrast to the resurrection narrative of Jesus being not there where he was killed and put away, sealed and secured, and where his disciples went to anoint/serve/adore him (as in the case of Mary) or seek him out (as in the case of Peter and John). He was rather already in the midst of those in the fringes of the earth by the seaside, those who could not be pushed any further from habitation but into the waters. Easter exposed this to the core, "He is not here; he has risen, just as he said … and is going ahead of you into Galilee" (Mt 28:6) indicating that Jesus can be met, will come alive, in places where two or three are gathered "in my name" (Mt 18:20)—in the context of mission, and never in the context of eulogising an event in history through liturgies of adoration and recital of creeds albeit salvific.

Covid therefore is a moment of truth that exposed *Christians* to the fact that Christianity is about being *Christlike* living out Jesus in neighbourhoods along with peoples of different faiths and beliefs, rather than seeking to be *'Christian'* as part of exclusivist faith communities that define 'faith' prejudicially and within parochial and even patriarchal hegemonic parameters of comfort. It is therefore pertinent to reboot as *ekklesia,* a called out people. And in this rebooting as the *ekklesia,* live out the Christian faith in neighbourhoods vis-à-vis being a gathered in and a gathering community. While engaging in meeting the needs of the people affected by the pandemic we did attempt being this *ekklesia*, of being Jesus in the neighbourhoods. However, attempts by the institutionalised church to bring online what was now 'providentially' forbidden within the four walls made us yearn for the comfort zones we were so accustomed to. There were only a few attempts by ecclesial-theological communities to seize the moment and attempt at radically deconstructing the monumental church.

The NCCI-CISRS webinar,[1] 'Learning to be the *Ekklesia* through the Context of the Corona', was one such attempt to help communities of faith reflect on the Covid-19 and post-Covid contexts and discern possible opportunities to be 'Christ-communities'. This offering was with the sincere hope that when it is possible to go back again into the familiar and into our religious places, we would reboot as *ekklesia* and will not do business as usual. A tall order, many say. Nevertheless a desire that the disciples of Jesus will reboot as Christ communities, as the *ekklesia*, and eventually deconstruct the exclusivist and excluding, hierarchical, patriarchal, imperialist church we were/are, living solely for ourselves and the perpetuation of an ecclesiastic-hierarchical legacy while faking to be missional. The corona context-lens leads us to discern a plethora of opportunities to live out Jesus.

Concern relating to people who have gone back to their locales is a case in point. Some call it reverse migration. A section of the media called this 'exodus without a promised land' little realising that they were going back to their own lands. We should be careful not to send them back to their neo-colonial masters, with the advice to 'be better slaves' as was also in the case of Onesimus who was fleeing from Philemon. The Church should take upon itself to sustain them in their own lands as entrepreneurs. In some cases it will be necessary to work on restoration of lands especially in the case of *panchami* lands or DC lands. It will also be important to think of appropriate use of the land that the Church Trusts hold on behalf of the people, whom they serve, including but not limited to such activities as community farming that affirm food security and sovereignty as well as assure job security. It will also be pertinent to plan how churches in urban centres will play host to people who are under compulsion to migrate to urban centres. We are not bereft of ideas but the resolve to address and engage.

Concerns relating to people with disability, mental health especially of young people and the growing generation, living sustainably with nature, promoting alternate and indigenous systems of medicine to address corporatisation of health and the monopoly of profit-oriented pharmaceutical companies, addressing gender based violence including domestic violence, sexual harassment, and all forms of child abuse, working on conflict transformation and learning to live in harmony with peoples of all faiths and beliefs, engaging with peoples of different sexual orientations and gender identities, responding to crises of losing jobs, rising rates of unemployment and underemployment, are some of the areas which needs to be addressed if and when we decide to reboot as *ekklesia*. In doing thus we need to also address economic imperialism which even during a life threatening pandemic supposedly values giving life to businesses rather than to addressing life itself.

It is therefore important that this rebooting also addresses the perils of money based economy vis-à-vis life oriented people-centred life giving life affirming economies even while living in those waters that negate it altogether—much like being 'in the world but not of the world'. The NCCI has initiated discussions on these by embarking on a series of initiatives under the 'rebooting as *ekklesia*' series including the webinars that are underway now.

Covid is a moment of truth. More importantly, it is a fleeting moment. Unless we seize the moment we are lost beyond redemption. Destroy this temple and in three days I will build it up, said Jesus. Unmindful of the movement of peoples that Jesus was seeking to build as the temple where God lives, we continue spending billions building temples where God doesn't live. This is only one example. A radical introspective theological task leading to life oriented missiological preoccupation and resultant ecclesiastic reconstruction is the call of the moment. Let us seize this fleeting moment and consider rebooting as a called out people rather than conducting business as usual, as a gathered-in and a gathering community.

Endnotes

[1] CISRS is the 'Centre for Indian Social Research and Studies', Bengaluru, India.

5

'Her Hands on the Threshold'

Will the Indian Church Give Witness in Post Covid Times?

Hemalatha John

---

1.   Introduction: Vulnerable Women during Lockdown

During the Covid-19 lockdowns, our world has been mute witness to the vilest of situations. UN Women reported that, "With lockdown, gender violence is a 'shadow pandemic': violence against women and girls, particularly domestic violence, has intensified."[1] Abuse and domestic violence against women and children has increased to a shocking extent. Several women have faced physical and psychological trauma. Indeed, while the poor suffer much more than those who have resources to tap during times of emergency, poor women, in particular, suffer the most. For instance, during the lockdown, many aged and weak women, as well as poor pregnant women were left with no food, shelter and basic care. Shockingly, an unnamed migrant labourer gave birth on the roadside with no medical care whatsoever. Scores of similar stories came to light through social media platforms.

The Church, like all other institutions in society, had to keep its doors physically closed during the lockdown. But, was the Church close to those who suffered? Was the Church silent or did it hear the voices of victims and respond? Although its doors were closed, did the Church—and, in future, how will the Church—get involved in pro-life activity? In all the misery and mess created by the pandemic, where is the safe place for weak and vulnerable women to flee and feel protected? This article will strive to throw some light on these questions seeking light from scripture, too.

2.　A Brief Look at the Covid-19 Crisis

Covid-19 has been a crisis with unprecedented and unimaginable consequences. There is no doubt that the corona virus has respected no territorial barriers but has wantonly affected the entire globe—not merely struck victims, but has laid low medicos, caretakers, so-called 'warriors' of Covid-19, families and the whole world, at large. In India in particular, Covid-19 played havoc on all the streams of life including the socio-politico-eco-spiritual support systems of individuals, and of society. Moreover, there have been many unnoticed and unreported struggles that poor people have been undergoing during lockdowns.

Focusing on the shattered Covid scenario, many people were critically evaluating the causes that triggered the pandemic and questioning: Is Covid-19 a case of bio-war as a result of power play among those with vested interests? Or, is it a natural calamity that can be understood by analysing the situation from a humanist, especially, a womanist perspective? Given this sad situation, what has been the response of the government, of educational institutions, and of religious centres for post care vigilance? It is beyond the scope of this article to provide answers to these questions. But, let us narrow our focus to see what has been and what can be a creative and committed response by the Church.

I think that during Covid-19, despite its locked doors, faith has been expressed and celebrated by the Church in India. Many local churches and their members across India identified with the needy to kindle in them a ray of hope. For instance, when the country was going through lockdowns, many migrant workers who were caught unaware and were unprepared found some refuge within church premises, with church organisations and Christian campuses that provided much-needed help. Archbishop Felix Machado of Bengaluru rightly said, "The church is always a mother, looking after her children, especially those in need, and in these special times, the church in India is indeed a Mother, providing for her children, the tribal, Dalit migrants."[2] Truly, reconciliation and restoration of life begin by being available at the right time and at the right place.

Now, in the light of a selected biblical text from the Book of Judges chapter 19, let us try to get some understanding of what is happening to people, especially to women, during this pandemic of unprecedented magnitude. Let us also ascertain how the closed doors of the Church can still remain as a threshold of hope for those who seek succour.

3.   The Levite and His Concubine: Textual Interpretation in a Covid Context

Will the politics of lockdown 2020 impact the Church and what role can the Church play to become a threshold of hope? From chapters 17-21 of the Book of Judges we understand that there was no king or leader in Israel; people lived according to their own whims and fancies without any proper political or administrative structure (17:6; 18:1; 19:1; 21:25). Chapter 19 narrates the story of a Levite who takes for himself a concubine. The narrative says, on the one hand, that when she was unfaithful, she went to her father's house in Bethlehem; however, on the other hand, nothing is said about how the Levite treated her; his integrity is not questioned.

3.1.   Victimisation of the Vulnerable: Home is a symbolic representation of safety, comfort and security, which provides people with a sense of belongingness. Moreover, when mention is made of a father's or mother's or parents' house, it does not only represent the ancestry of a person, rather, it denotes personal identity. Therefore, when the concubine returns to her father's home, she is seeking security, acceptance and identity.

As the narrative progresses, we are told that the Levite goes to his concubine's father's house in Bethlehem to bring her back to Ephraim. There he is treated with great honour and hospitality by the woman's father. He then begins his journey of return with his concubine and his servant. In all this, the concubine is silent for the Levite never seeks her opinion. However, when there is need for a halt during transit at Gib-e-ah, the Levite takes the opinion of his servant. They are given a place to eat and rest by a generous host: an old man. Meanwhile, a group of perverse Gibites surround the old man's house and demand that he sends the Levite out to them for their sexual pleasure and indulgence. The host refuses to send the 'male Ephraimite Levite' out, saying: "Do not act so wickedly. Since this man is my guest, do not do this vile thing. Here are my virgin daughter and his concubine. Ravish them and do whatever you want to them" (vv.23-24).

It is shocking that the host is willing to send his virgin daughter and Levite's concubine in order to safeguard the Levite. The host's concern is only the Levite. In order to safeguard patriarchal religious, sexual and societal norms, a virgin and the Levite's concubine are pushed out of the house for the sexual pleasure of some men. This act is an inferior politics of dishonoring woman: victimisation of the vulnerable. While the Levite and the woman were both seeking protection behind locked doors, the Levite stayed safe; not the woman.

3.2. Resistance of the Vulnerable: The Levite's concubine becomes the victim (Judg 19:25-26). The Levite seizing and pushing her out to the abusers indicates defence politics at the cost of her life. When the Gibite abusers let her go after molesting her through the night, it is daybreak. "As morning appeared, the woman came and fell down at the door of the man's house where her master was, until it was light." (v.26). The concubine reaches the door of the house and holds the threshold of the door from where she was pushed. Earlier, her first return was to her father's home and then she is sent back to the Levite's house. This is now her second return after the Levite has pushed her out to be victimised by the sexual abusers. Although she is a victim of social, religious and sexual norms, she still continues seeking security and resisting the act of victimisation by returning home and holding the threshold.

The woman's outstretched hands symbolically represent fighting back from her vulnerable condition and a bid to return and seek security. Despite her struggle to return, the Levite cut her into twelve pieces sending them to the tribes of Israel to explain the scenario of victimisation of the vulnerable and her return home. The holding of the threshold represents resistance of the vulnerable to establish justice. Her act of resistance continued to make the nation realize the significance of leadership.

The phrase 'hands on the threshold' indicates that the concubine came back to the relationship and the place of security even though the Levite seized and surrendered her to perverse men. She came back to seek protection and to be assured that she would be accepted into the household. Sadly, when the door opened up to the light, she neither got any protection nor any assurance. The politics of honour, power and defence prevailed. There was no respect for her life, no honour given to her even in death. The brutality of the Levite is condoned.

4. Conclusion: Church Called to be a Threshold of Hope

Covid-19 is a serious pandemic condition affecting the whole world. The struggle to defend life will be an ongoing challenge. The affected seek a place of healing with hope, which includes restoring life and providing post-medical care. Today, the Indian Church has become a threshold to the vulnerable, particularly for women in the Covid-19 crisis. There are innumerable hands striving to reach the threshold of the Church. These outstretched hands beg for security and resistance against vulnerability. What is, and will be, the response of the Indian Church? Will the Church try to avoid strangers, resort to denominationalism and glorify the traditions and doctrines as defence politics or will it participate in the Nazareth Manifesto? (Lk 4:16-18).

The power play of the pandemic has victimized innocent lives with many playing games behind closed doors. How can the Church become a resting place, a threshold of hope and security? The true nature of the Church is to care for the vulnerable (1 Tim 5:16-17). Church is not only a building but the life-protecting and life-sustaining Body of Jesus Christ. God's dwelling cannot be confined within churches of mortar and bricks built by human hands (Acts 7:48); but God dwells among people (Rev 21:3). May Church be a place of threshold—allowing people to come in for the help and healing. May the Church be open for all exigencies that may arise for this unprecedented pandemic!

Endnotes

[1] The Hindu newspaper reported on May 17, 2020.

[2] https://cruxnow.com/church-in-asia/2020/04/india-church-focuses-on-marginalized-migrants-during-coronavirus-lockdown/

6

The Tormented Truth:
Hope as the Paradox of Despair

Packiam T. Samuel

"They owe nothing to anyone but everything to the dead." So writes Elie Wiesel, the most celebrated memorialist of the survivors of the Holocaust. One could begin nowhere else. It is Covid-19 which determines the universe of thought right now, both as that which must be comprehended in all its incomprehensibility and as the unanswerable accusation which must nevertheless be answered. The survivors whose voice we make our own are condemned to survive within a mystery we can never resolve. The capacity in which we live spells a necessity never to let die the name and fate of those who did. The future is in thrall to that past. From this necessity time brings no reprieve. For the surviving generations will have this etched in their memory.

The lockdown imposed across the entire globe due to Covid-19 has brought out our glaring abuse of nature. In the post-pandemic era, as survival of human species is threatened, we will have learnt under global lockdown that as human activity came to a grinding halt, the planet earth and myriad life forms were refreshed, rejuvenated and flourished. For billions of living organisms on the planet it surely is party time! Within a month of the lockdown, in two hundred and twenty countries the gaping hole in the ozone layer has healed herself, pink flamingos from the Rann of Kutch have returned to the swamp lands of Navi Mumbai, hordes of wild deer are crossing the national highways, air pollution levels in New Delhi and other Metros has come down to healthy levels, noise pollution decibels have disappeared too! Scientists point out, for example, rising global warming had gotten temperatures to rise in the Arctic region causing extensive meltdown of ice releasing different kinds of viruses into fresh waters hitherto frozen and locked for millions of years.

Scientists are puzzled also with the versatility of the corona virus for the way it has mutated itself in so many different ways adapting to vagaries of climatic and other geographical conditions in two hundred and twenty countries. Moreover, we are told to prepare ourselves to live with Covid for another two hundred years, if not more! Thus, it is right also that we should begin with debt, inexorable and unremitting, and see the writing as its partial payment, a homage to the victims and an incrimination of the world. No matter how utterly unmatched Covid-19 may be, no matter how far beyond all precedents of calamity, it belongs with the unity of humanity. To this unity, however shattered, appeal is made most ardently where it is most bitterly denied. Such is 'the torment of truth': Christian, Hindu, Islamic or any other.

In 'owing everything to the dead and nothing to anyone', the survivors are creditors of the rest of humanity, awaiting the hope of payment of the debts of guilt, of repentance and honesty, of truth. If it were not so, there could be no literature of the Covid-19, but only the silence of the dead. From a world incapable of heeding there could be only heedlessness. The whole thrust of accusation falls away unless it is also a surge of hope. There is a will to faith in the very passion of unbelief. In all their grimness, Covid-19 writings have to be read as strenuous appeal. It is a seeking, as well as a searing, eloquence. It has to do with the enormous indebtedness of the world and demands to have it paid. Despair that it can be, only intensifies the claim.

This dimension of tormented truth, of hope as the paradox of despair, now onwards will mark all our work and influence. It makes us a foremost protagonist of the central theme in interfaith relations in our time. In all its proper vehemence, there is a prosecutor's search for hope. The indictment cannot hold without the faith that can identify its ground in the truth. That truth is not only stark event; it is also human community the more insistent in being the more violated. Covid-19 overwhelms all normal landmarks in human history in all ordinary logic. They do so not only in what they are but in what they bequeath. Their legacies rightly perpetuate their agonies. In giving voice to this quality of things past and things present.

Everything proceeded as if the poor and at present the migrant in particular did not, should not, must not, exist. Where, then, was the covenant, the mutual inter-necessity of God and God's people? With all these dead before our eyes, I am afraid to stumble over my own, our urge is to throw away the pen, burn all bridges and start to run and curse.

Can there be a Christian, Hindu, Islamic, or any other, theology after the Covid-19 pandemic? Was there not a total treachery in that callous non-intervention from on High? The question that we must pose to God becomes in reverse the question God poses to us—the enigma of betrayal interrogating the enigma of annihilation. But for the Covid-19, myself would have been a pious student, labouring devoutly over conferences, and symposium after symposium, giving talks on interfaith, not the present passionate searcher after the credibility of God.

To doubt may be to deny, but it is also to await and to await with the ultimate criterion of what must be awaited— an awareness to commensurate with what has to be made to mean. There are times when the only option is to conclude the ancient covenant utterly foregone, shattered in the ashes of the crematoria. There are other times when, phoenix-like, faith must remake a covenantal relationship with God, only thereby not to be posthumously defeated by Covid.

So, to conclude does not diminish, ignore or fail to comprehend Covid-19. Nor does it weaken the imperative to have it ever memorialised. On the contrary, it goes to the heart of 'the torment of the truth' of it. This may not be the same question as the viability of the covenant and a theodicy of unfailing election. For these there are all the resources of our fidelity to God. The Cross is a discernible answer to a different question, namely, how in an economy we can attribute to God, evil is made to yield to love via the suffering in which they meet. The other question is whether the answer can have its paradigm in a history where it is disclosed, transacted and confirmed, so that we can live in its light.

States, cultures, peoples, all collectives, will still need sinews, defenses, advocates, protagonists of justice and truth. The scientist's truth, historian's truth, the poet's truth, the statesman's truth, the moralist's truth, all these are to be strenuously sought and served. Otherwise, the evils are neither identified nor recognised, and, therefore, not confronted. But the final truth of our solidarity in human is its meaning in suffering interpreted by the love of God.

As we get over the intensity of the onslaught of the present pandemic, we humans need to bend and correct our lifestyles in critical ways. If not, the next pandemic may wipe us out from the planet, so that our counter parts: namely, other billions of life forms may thrive and multiply and inherit the planet earth for themselves.

To sum up, the Covid-19 pandemic reminds us that we are—deep down—spiritual beings, whether we realise it or not, and makes us recognise that the problem of corona virus is right here embedded in the lungs of our global community. This is a challenge that requires global cooperation and unity, a component of compassion to alleviate suffering, and a greater responsibility to exercise our faith to witness divine intervention. Though the Covid-19 crisis has brought the world to a halt; and sadly, the health and economic impact will be disastrous, I feel that from a spiritual angle, the pros will outweigh the cons making us a global community with spiritual connectivity.

7

Covid-19 and Concerns of Health Care

Sunil Caleb

The Context: Covid-19 Closedown of Private Clinics

One of the strangest sights in Kolkata that I have seen after the corona virus pandemic began is the shut doors of the private doctors' clinics that just the other day used to be full of patients waiting to consult the doctors. A doctor who used to be regularly consulted by our college students was unavailable on the mobile phone when an emergency came up. When late at night we went to a mission hospital we fortunately found the Emergency open but the hospital was unable to admit the patient until a corona virus test was carried out. Another person who came to a private hospital for cancer treatment caught the corona virus and unfortunately succumbed to it.

Used to dealing with non-emergency non-infectious diseases and procedures of relatively better off persons, the doctors and hospitals in the private sector have been of little use when the pandemic struck. In fact, feeling threatened by the fact that persons coming for treatment for the usual sicknesses and procedures might be infected with the corona virus and hence infect other patients and health care workers (HCWs), some private hospitals have just decided to play safe and try to ride out the storm by totally shutting down their OPDs and indoor patient facilities. Other hospitals that have set apart facilities for the treatment of Covid-19 patients have been accused of giving huge bills to the patients who are admitted to the private hospitals.

Limitations of Private Health Care

When these shortcomings of private health care are pointed out, I am not arguing that the private health care providers are somehow wicked and sinful people. No, the providers are only behaving rationally in the context of how private health care works. All providers of health care in the private sector (which is almost entirely based on the profit motive) are acting in reasonable and rational ways given the way that the private health care system functions. Unless these private health care providers earn an income that is higher than their costs they will not survive for long. So in the face of the corona pandemic, it makes eminent economic sense for them to take actions like stopping seeing patients, closing down clinics and nursing homes and so on. If the doctor has the clinic open it is obvious that s/he will attract sick people, many of whom may be infected with the corona virus.

The fact that the corona virus is highly infectious and easily transmittable (through droplets emitted from coughing or even normal speaking) means that the private doctor cannot take the risk of seeing more than one patient at a time and cannot allow the patients waiting to see her or him to be within six feet of one another. For private medical practitioners, having a small clinic, this is too expensive and therefore impractical. Making provision for physical distancing is hugely expensive and so the doctor just closes down her or his clinic even if the doctor is specialized in an area of medicine that was unlikely to attract patients with symptoms of being affected with corona virus, (like piles for instance). Similarly, most private hospitals find it too costly to make the changes needed to treat Covid-19 patients, and they have HCWs who are too afraid of contracting the virus and so just only treat no-Covid-19 patients after asking every potential patient to go through a test to establish that they do not have the virus.

The result of this shutting down a lot of the private health care facilities at this time of Covid-19 pandemic when actually they are more needed (people have not stopped having heart problems, kidney stones, TB and so on) shows us that privatised health care is really not a good way of running a programme that provides health and healing to all the kinds of diseases that are present in our world today. It might not be a problem to have private doctors who undertake plastic surgery, but private doctors find it impossible to do their jobs in an infectious disease pandemic.

The corona pandemic has shown us that "All are not safe until everyone is safe," or "All are not protected until everyone is treated." If this is the post-Covid 19 reality, it is obvious that in future, health care cannot just be about curative care but must be more about preventive health and public health. Our country cannot just wait for the next outbreak of a very infectious disease like Covid-19 which has no known cure—which, with deforestation and climate change, is said to be just a matter of time—before taking action to increase its public health capacity, but must begin now. Private health care cannot, almost by definition, undertake the actions needed to test, trace, track and treat the spread of the virus. This is for economic reasons, for no one will pay to be forcibly tested and quarantined. Such actions can only be done by the state.

Another area where privatised health care falls far short of what consists of satisfactory health care in the post corona virus world, emerges in the pharmaceutical area. The development of a vaccine against the corona virus is crucial for enabling the opening up of the economy and enabling people to meet in close quarters. Many efforts are being made to develop a vaccine, some in university labs and some in private pharmaceutical labs. Once the vaccine is available, the question will be how will it be distributed, at what cost and who will be given the vaccine first (given that it will take time to produce enough doses to vaccinate practically the whole population of the world)? If the development of the vaccine is done by a private pharmaceutical company that decides to make a profit, it is very likely that the vaccine will be first available only in the wealthy nations of the world and perhaps, there too, only available to those who can afford it. This will mean that the already wealthy will be able to go back to work and earn income faster than the poorer people. This will quite obviously increase the inequalities that already exist.

Responsibility of the Public Health Authorities towards the Poor

In the light of the above mentioned reasons, it is essential that development and the distribution of the vaccine for corona virus be somehow handled by either the World Health Organization or some new multi-lateral organisation where there are representatives of less-developed countries. If the private pharma companies are allowed to sell the corona virus vaccine it is obvious that they will sell the vaccine on the basis of who can pay for the vaccine. They might even auction the rights to manufacture the vaccine to the highest bidder, though given the huge damage this path might do to the reputation of the discoverer of the vaccine, it is unlikely to happen. However, given the responsibility of companies to make profits for their shareholders, even if good individuals within a pharma company wanted to give the vaccine to the poor, they cannot, without losing their jobs. This will then surely mean that the needy poor will only get the vaccine much later, after the richer countries and the rich within the poor countries have bought it. This injustice in distribution of the vaccine will cause the existing inequalities between the poor and the wealthy to increase. Hence it is essential that the vaccine is distributed according to the risk that people have from contracting the virus, with those at high risk receiving the vaccine than those at a lower risk. Such a pattern of distribution can only be handled by a public health authority and not by the private sector. Hence the post-Covid-19 world must see a large jump in public spending on health and perhaps a down-grading of the private sector.

II
TOMORROW'S CORONA OF LIFE?

8

The Making of the Future: Insights from the Young

Vinod Victor

Viewing the Pandemic from the Perspective of Youth

Another pandemic has made its presence felt. Breaking through the most sophisticated of defence mechanisms it played havoc with normal life in almost every nation. Medical science with all its claims of postmodern advancements stood next to helpless. Governments tried all that was humanly possible to contain the virus and health care systems doled out the best they could. Yet the pandemic found its own ways of penetrating newer areas. The jargon of the people changed. Alongside fighting the virus, we should now learn to live with the virus they said. Returning to the normal to which the world was used to might be a distant reality they claimed and therefore called everyone to prepare for the 'new-normal'. Even as researchers plunged into the possibilities of the new future, the young people also engaged in a debate as to how the re-boot could affect their understanding and envisioning of the church and the future.

Of the many ways human wisdom thought of to mitigate the impact of the pandemic one was a total lockdown. Life all over was paralysed. Public gatherings were prohibited by new laws and ordinances. All religious, social and cultural gatherings of people were banned. The economic fabrics that held life together started falling off the tapestry. With 'Stay Home' being the slogan of the lockdown people started asking: Where is Home? Several people who realised they were strangers where they were, longed to return home. Along with deaths and brutal exposing of the limitations of health care mechanisms the world had to deal with people on the move. Reverse-migration, quarantines, Covid protocols and inexplicable pain and agony marked life everywhere. This was the context in which the youngsters envisioned the future they wanted to participate in the making.

Digital Presence and Dismal Absence

When physical coming together was not possible the Church like any other institution found alternate ways to be functional within the limitations. Church services began to be live streamed and premiered. New digital platforms zoomed in for people to meet. There was an initial interest with people taking part with great enthusiasm. Virtual meetings, virtual choirs and even virtual eucharist was being debated and experimented. Digital giving was encouraged.

Young people found new and creative ways of mastering the quarantine and keeping their interest level going. But a mere fifty days later there were three basic realisations: one, digital church can never be the replacement of real physical church, two, the digital exclusion of several people is something which could be an irrecoverable loss and three, the digital fatigue could be much more complex than was originally thought of and sustaining interest in the digital church could be very challenging specially among the younger and older folks. Statistics might point towards a surge in viewership of online telecasts and podcasts—the same being available to a larger clientele—but a survey among regular church goers points to the fact that less than fifty percent are digitally engaged with the efforts taken to be active.

Much more than the creative attempts to be present the younger people were disappointed with the dismal absence of the Church at such a time as this. The death of dear ones across the world globally, the stress and trauma in being tested positive, the struggle of the diaspora and the migrant workers to reach home, the existential angst that has gripped every walk of life including those being quarantined and living in hotspots and red zones, the pain of the people deprived of their livelihood, the clandestine efforts of some administrations to use the opportunity to push their agenda, the panorama view of the present include all these and much more. This was the time when the prophetic voice of the Church and the justice involvement should have been most vociferously heard and seen. However, the absence at such a time as this and the satisfaction in minimal engagement like a few food kits, masks and a contribution to a relief fund is something history will not see lightly.

The opportunities that the pandemic opened up for mission and ministry and to assert the presence is being dismally missed out by the Church both locally and universally.

The young people opine that much more can be and should be done lest the generations to come will point to this time and say: "the Church was missing in action" — this not belittling the genuine and wonderful work some of the churches and religious institutions were engaged in during this time.

Faith Factor and the Fear Factor

When can I go and meet with the Lord in God's house? This prayer of Psalm 42:2 seems to be in the mind of several young people who confess to already having nostalgia about being back in the pews soon. Will normalcy be restored when lockdowns are lifted? Some young people say that it could take quite some time for the mask and the distance protocols to be lifted from ordinary lives if at all they would be lifted.

Pastoral visits and pastoral engagements the youth point out could be very different with the regular visits to homes finding limitations with the new protocols for safety being drawn up. Marriages and burials will continue to have controls in number. Many of the social activities that marked the beauty of church life might never return. However, this also provides an opportunity to do away with several of the rites and rituals that have become very redundant in the eyes of the young people.

Of the fear factors, the most important one the religious communities will have to learn to cope with would be nosophobia: the fear of contracting an infectious disease. This could have manifold implications including an urge to keep away from community and even if in community a fear of the other as a potential source of the disease. The sharing of peace and even the eucharist will be seen with great doubt and fear. A new kind of fear *geitonaphobia*: fear of the neighbour could grip many believers.

Most people of the new generation have their faith in God intact and have not lost their confidence in science and technology. They believe a way out of the pandemic would soon be found—be it a successful treatment or a vaccine and the threat from the virus could also be a non-existential reality soon. Those who believe that Covid-19 is a biological weapon also seem to hold the view the perpetrators would already have the panacea that could hit the markets soon.

This could also be a time the Church spends in self-reflection identifying the essentials and non-essentials for the future. The ecumenical movement survived without travels but not losing the connect with each other. Webinars and modern versions of e-meetings replaced major global events. With resource crunch the most prudent ways of investing available resources and commitment to optimal use could also mark a major shift in the diakonia and witness of the faith of the Church.

Inclusion and Exclusion

With every cross section of life being affected, the pertinent question during the pandemic is: who is the most affected? While the Church affirms solidarity with the last, the lost and the least, a clear ecclesial and social audit of the last hundred days of the life of the Church and mapping disability inclusion, digitally deprived peoples care, socially ostracised persons and vulnerable people groups ministry focus, the new positive people's trauma management protocols and the Covid response systems and mechanisms put in place would in no doubt not be in vain to have a clearer focus for the future. The physical, emotional, economic, psychological, mental, spiritual, social and wholistic well-being of the post Covid world will urge the Church to a new renewal and an inevitable reformation.

With the homes becoming sanctuaries during the lockdown the new inclusion in the worship pattern, i.e., the priesthood of all believers, with women taking the lead in several homes, could sustain the spiritual life of homes, the basic unit of the ecclesia, for quite some time to come. If properly followed up, this could address major exclusions the Church was grappling with, finding no easy solutions.

The new markings of exclusion the positive people suffer is only a pointer to the shifts in the purity-pollution constructs so deep rooted in the collective consciousness of the Church and Society, at large. This kairotic time could be used to yet again 'name' those realities the Church needs to be redeemed from. The excluded should be re-identified and inclusion should become the mark of the future of the Church. The positive impact on the environment of the lockdown and rest should also be a major learning as to how creation care should be included more in the agenda of the ecclesia and of the future making initiatives.

Conclusion: Young, and Ready to Tread the Road Less Travelled

The young people continue to affirm that the future we are waiting for will not refrain from learning from the mistakes of the past, will not shy away from course corrections wherever there are realisations of the wrong roads taken and will refocus on the kingdom that the Lord of Light and Life has promised to usher in. The present situation is only a trigger to ensure that the journey towards the future of God is not derailed by human lacuna.

9

Rebirthing Church on the Model of the Early Christian Community

Shalini Mulackal

Introduction: Covid, Confusion and the Call for Conversion

We are living in a world fighting a pandemic caused by Covid-19. It has spread to almost all the countries of the world. Experts say that the world will never be the same again after this pandemic which has gripped all the countries and continents without any discrimination.

The origin of this virus still remains a mystery. Many hypotheses are being proposed and publicised. Was this virus produced in a laboratory in Wuhan? If so, for what purpose? Was it a consequence of Wuhan being the first city to be covered completely by 5-G spectrum? If so, the virus could be nothing but the poisoned or damaged cells excreted from human bodies which were exposed to the high radiation. Or did the virus originate in a wet market as China claims? Whatever be the answer, one thing is certain: our human interference in nature beyond any limits and our increasing alienation from it has caused this pandemic.

Covid-19 has changed our world radically. We have been mute witnesses to the collapse of national and world economies, the breakdown of relationships among nations, questioning the credibility of even a once-respected international body like the WHO, loss of employment for millions of people worldwide, the sudden visibility of millions of migrant workers and their plight under an ill-planned lockdown and millions of others struggling for survival. The institutional church too has experienced its limitations in a big way as the churches still remain shut for more than three months as of now. Worship in a large congregation is not only seen as non-essential but has also become a threat to public health!

This is the first time ever since Christianity organised itself as an institution that Christians were forced to stay at home and not participate in the liturgical services and avail of other sacraments. Of course, many churches took the help of internet to have virtual liturgical services. It is in this scenario that we need to envision a post Covid-19 Church. There is a clarion call to rebirth a new Church according to the model of the early Christian community. We need a new Pentecost. This is a time for introspection and change. It is a time to respond to the ever-new call of the Gospel, *metanoiate,* be converted!

Christ, Koinonia and Community

Christianity is a religion of communities. It is clear from the four Gospels that Jesus and his disciples formed an itinerant community that had no place to claim as their own (Mt 8:20). The community was not only of the twelve apostles but also others including women who accompanied them from Galilee to Jerusalem (Lk 8:1-3). It was an inclusive community. At the time of Pentecost, the origins of the Church, when the Holy Spirit descended upon the disciples, there were women present in the group praying together with Mary, the Mother of Jesus (Acts 1:12-14, 2:1-4). And all of them received the same gift of the Holy Spirit.

The early Christians too were referred to as a community holding everything in common (Acts 2:42-47; 4:32-37). Paul, the apostle to the Gentiles, reiterates the same idea of an egalitarian and inclusive community in his Letter to the Galatians (3:28). However, this original vision was somewhat lost when Emperor Constantine made Christianity the official state religion. Gradually Christianity, which began as a movement, became the institutional Church. As structures of the Church solidified little by little, the female members of the Church found themselves on the fringes of the institution and were treated more as consumers of spiritual goods which a male-centred, clerical Church had to offer.

The Church in 2020 looks very different from the early Christian community in their way of responding to the risen Christ and expressing their belief and commitment to him. While in the early Christian community, there was no needy person among the believers, we have today the *haves* and the *have nots.* Instead of *fellowship* we have divisions among us based on caste, sex, culture, language, doctrine and style of worship. Instead of coming together to pray and to break bread in memory of Jesus, we have built up structures that negate and exclude the egalitarian vision of the Reign of God.

As a result, we have churches primarily with a male face. The female face is nearly absent from public view. This is evident in public discussions, panels, debates, seminars and ecumenical prayers where women are either absent or are given only a token representation. With the invisibility of the female, the feminine dimensions too are relegated to the background. Within the present structures of the Church there is no way women can be given visibility. For this to happen we need new structures which takes seriously the equal discipleship of women.

A Mother Church is Possible

We need to build up from the ground reality. It is usually women as mothers who inculcate and nurture the faith in their children. It is they who gather all the members together for family prayers. It is women who take the lead whenever there are families in the neighbourhood coming together to pray and share the Word of God. It is women who take responsibility in executing many of the parish activities.

The post Covid-19 churches I envisage are small neighbourhood communities where women play an equal role in fulfilling their baptismal call of teaching, sanctifying and governing. I envisage a Church which emphasises the common priesthood of all believers rather than magnifying the ministerial priesthood. The ministerial priesthood is at the service of the common priesthood of people.

The parish community which will be a communion of many neighbourhood communities can gather for certain occasions. Bearing witness to Christian life needs to take place at the neighbourhood communities. In these household churches, the members make sure that there is no needy person among them. They choose their own leaders and gather regularly in the name of Jesus, to share the Word of God and to break bread in His memory. In such neighbourhood communities it will be possible to invite people of other faiths too occasionally who are one's neighbours.

Conclusion: Rebirthing a More Inclusive and Responsive Church

Rebirthing of such a Church requires that all Christians get help in faith formation, biblical interpretation and are not solely dependent on the ordained clergy. The people, men and women, mothers and fathers, grandmothers and grandfathers need to be trained and empowered to interpret the Word of God from their own unique experiences. The post Covid-19 Church therefore is not a clergy dependent Church but a Church where there will be much more participation of all Christians. Here, the baptised are enabled to live their Christian life as adult Christians taking much more responsibility. It will be a Church where women too are accepted and treated as equal disciples of Jesus.

10

Renewing Faith in God and in God's Family in Covid Times

Francis Gonsalves

Introduction: Covid-19 and the Silence of God

"I'm waiting for this pandemic to end so that I can resume my ministry of healing and miracle-working!" ran a sarcastic WhatsApp message I received. Today, not only have faith-healers gone silent, but God is put in the dock. Where is God? How does God allow these deaths? On the one hand, the Covid-19 pandemic has smashed our certainties and securities, and on the other, the lockdown opens up to new times and fresh thinking. Let's reflect upon our faith, church, ministry and family life. Most importantly, we must renew our faith in a God who seems asleep while millions worldwide are weak, weary and worn out as never before.

In this article, I will first show how believers in two major world religions—Christianity and Hinduism—have done more disservice than good on account of their blind belief.

Second, I shall offer some reflections on how we can renew our faith in God and God's Family, at large.

Playing God and Manipulating Myths

Christian fundamentalists often endanger life rather than promote it. A young pastor from Cameroon died of Covid-19 on May 16 after preaching that faith and the laying on of his hands would ward off the corona virus. His death sent hundreds of his followers berserk, blocking his burial, since they believed he would rise again. One of his followers, said: "If you, the person that claims that you are curing Covid-19, are dead, what about others affected by Covid-19? I do not know how the people that he was laying hands on will be healed."[1] Like this bogus faith-healer, there are scores of prophets of doom mouthing Bible verses, waxing eloquence about God's wrath and the end of the world. Fanatics do more harm than good to their followers.

Hinduism—the majority religion in India—plays a massive role in moulding public opinion. The pandemic got politicians and religionists wedded to Hindutva ideology using religion to calm public fear, with little success. The immensely popular Ramayana and Mahabharat epics were televised not only to keep devotees at home, but had leaders predicting that while the Mahabharata war was won in eighteen days, India would win its war against Covid-19 in twenty-one. This historicising of myths went in vain.

Likewise, members of the Akhil Bharat Hindu Mahasabha conducted a *gaumutra* (cow urine) drinking ritual near a temple at Delhi's Mandir Marg on March 14. A banner bearing the image of a demon with 'Corona' painted across its chest was displayed and a sadhu performed a ritual chanting: "Corona *shant ho jao, shant ho jao,* corona!"—meaning, 'calm down, Corona'! Thereafter, all present drank *gaumutra.*[2] Obviously, all these sham godmen are red-faced now.

Called to Review our Images of God and Renew Our Family Life

Learning from our mistakes, let's review: (a) our understanding of God; (b) our life in family; (c) our relationship with mother earth and her poor children.

God created us in the divine image and likeness (Gen 1:26-27) but we seek to replace God with idols of *our* image and likeness. The Great *"I Am Who I Am"* (Ex 3:14) who revealed Godself to Moses and led the chosen people with mighty signs and wonders from slavery to freedom is the incarnate God in Jesus. Jesus' *"I Am"* sayings—bread of life; light of the world; door of the sheep; good shepherd; the resurrection and the life; the way, the truth and the life; and the true vine—should reassure us that only He is Lord and Master of our earthly life, and resurrection, thereafter. Jesus' death and resurrection do not remove suffering and pain but give them new meaning.

If God's Son, Jesus, bore a 'corona' of thorns—*corona,* meaning 'crown' in Latin—at his passion and death, isn't it alright if God allows His children to bear one, today, too? After all, doesn't God also promise the "crown of life" to those who are faithful, persevere and love God? (Jas 1:12; Rev 2:10). We know not what the future holds for us, but we do know *who* holds that future. So, rather than play god, let us surrender with deep faith and trust. God knows what is best for you and for me.

On the home front, Covid-19 has got us 'homebound'. The pressures and pleasures of our world earlier forced us to move out and move around the world at a dizzying pace. For many, there was little difference between home and hotel, except that one got free food and bedrest in the former. Now that lockdowns have forced one to stay indoors, there seem to be positive effects of being homebound. Being 'bound' can be understood negatively as being confined; but 'home-bound' also has a positive side with the home-bonds of love, service, caring, sharing and self-sacrifice fortified through more interactions among family members.

Family life also has a depth dimension. The psalmist says: "Be still and know that I am God" (Ps 45:10). Homebound, many have found time to be 'at home' with God, savouring God's paternal protection and maternal care. Many families have found time to pray together and to be present as family at online prayer and worship services. Many realise that God is not just 'up there' in the heavens nor 'out there' in the church; but is Emmanuel: God-is-with-us (Mt 1:23). Praying at home has made the family more aware of being a 'domestic church' and temple of the Spirit.

One member of our family who we often forget and badly abuse is mother earth. Everyone knows the perilous plight of our planet. In 2015, Pope Francis published an encyclical entitled 'Laudato Si'—Italian, *Praise be!*[3]—referring to the 'Canticle of Creatures' of St Francis of Assisi, who "reminds us that our common home is like a sister with whom we share our life and a beautiful mother who opens her arms to embrace us." Do we really treat our earth as a sister and a mother? Our *'oikos'* or 'home' embraces three realms of life: ecology, economics and ecumenism. There is urgent need to see how these three interact with each other and what possibilities they present for those most in need.

Dreaming of a "poor church for the poor", in n.49 of *Laudato Si'* Pope Francis wrote, "We have to realize that a true ecological approach *always* becomes a social approach; it must integrate questions of justice in debates on the environment, so as to hear *both the cry of the earth and the cry of the poor.*" Viruses thrive due to ecological abuses and imbalances; yet, those who suffer most are the poorest of poor who, ironically, are neither guilty of excessive consumption nor of disdain for mother nature.

The lockdown has been disastrous for the poorest of poor: daily wage earners, unskilled labourers and underpaid youth who found themselves homeless, jobless and cashless. Suddenly, thousands of aged citizens, pregnant women, and little children began walking barefoot in the scorching summer to their homes hundreds of miles away. Aren't they our mothers, sisters and children? Did we, as Church, respond adequately to this catastrophe of unimaginable proportion?

Conclusion: Towards a New Heaven and a New Earth

One never knows what will happen post-pandemic. Our lives have always been more abnormal than normal. Can we hope that things get 'normal'? Hardly. All we say is: Let God be God. Jesus warns us that someday we'll hear the words: "Whatever you did—or did not do—to the least of my sisters and brothers, you did—or did not do—to me" (Mt 25:40,45). While taking care of our family members let's not forget these '*least*' of God's Family. Finally, let's move forward with God's Spirit and cooperate with the One who says: "See I am making all things new" (Rev 21:5).

Endnotes

[1] https://www.huffingtonpost.in/entry/frankline-ndifor-pastor-cameroon_n_5ec60a00c5b6dfc078e0f7ee?ri18n=true accessed on May 24, 2020.

[2] See https://caravanmagazine.in/religion/hindutva-groups-cow-urine-protection-covid19 accessed on May 25, 2020.

[3] See http://www.vatican.va/content/francesco/en/encyclicals/documents/papa-francesco_20150524_enciclica-laudato-si.html for the text; accessed on May 26, 2020.

11

The 'Butterfly Effect' and Cosmic Interconnectedness

Philip Kuruvilla

Butterfly Effect and Post-Pandemic Church

Many of us may not have read *science fiction*, more popularly called 'sci- fi'. In 1952, American Ray Bradbury wrote a sci-fi short story titled: '*A Sound of Thunder*' about time travel a century later, in 2055. This is often credited as the origin of the term '*butterfly effect*'. Bradbury illustrated how the death of a butterfly millions of years in the past could have drastic changes in the future. The term became more widely known after MIT mathematician, Edward Lorenz, delivered a lecture in 1972 entitled: "*Predictability: Does the Flap of a Butterfly's Wings in Brazil Set Off a Tornado in Texas?*" He held that tiny changes might result in unpredictable effects, but he also opined that our ability to analyse and predict the functioning of the world is inherently limited. How then can we envision or predict a post-Covid Church?

I'd like to take an IT phrase for examination. My observation is that the modern concept of the *Internet of Things (IoT)* is better represented as *the Interconnectedness of Things,* and Covid-19 should have made us realise that; unfortunately, it has not. Officially the term captures the future of device-to-device interaction and how we, as users of these devices, expect an interconnected, always-on, world to respond to our needs and desires.

A 'conceptual perspective' of the *Interconnectedness of Things* is the idea of devices detecting and responding to actions and changes in context without human intervention. This concept is more than the lights turning off when no one is in the room—that's a single device operating in a single context. Think instead of many worldly actions with many contexts. Think instead, totally unconnected happenings which ultimately bring about cataclysmic changes in our lives, but which also bring us to the knowledge of our common existence as the human species. This may help us discuss the place that the Church has in our post-Covid lives, and the changes that need to be introduced to make it once more the 'Bride of Christ' through its relevance and holiness.

Thinking of a post-Covid Church is nothing new. All around us different groups in society are working out the 'new normal' of the post-Covid world. Many concerned people ask: What would life be like in a post-Covid society? Others are apprehensive and argue about political structures, economic impacts, labour and migration, paradigm shifts in literature, sport and art—all these spheres which touch our lives, each one being important. It is therefore quite natural for faith groups and faith leaders to envision the future of their faith communities. Christian leaders, too, are considering how to best contain the far-reaching effects—both negative and positive—of the pandemic. Predictions are already being made of how the Church will change more permanently in the way it functions post-pandemic, if it learns lessons from the present and tries to prepare for future emergencies. Life is certainly not going to be the same after the pandemic. But greater and faster-than-before changes will happen in Church and in the secular world. We need to understand and to chalk out our priorities and engagement levels with the tenets of Christianity.

Mapping Milestones for the Church's Future Mission

I came across an insightful article: "Ten Ways the Post-Covid Church will be Different" by Fr Joshan Rodrigues in *Indian Catholic Matters* [ICM], published on April 24, 2020. I would like to share *some* of his headlines which I felt were relevant, but have added my own inputs to better suit the readers of this article.

1. 'Household churches': According to the Acts of the Apostles, the earliest Christians worshipped in house-churches. The lockdown has exposed the weaknesses of a church building-centric model that we are accustomed to, and which has failed, and which can fail in situations like these or during natural disasters. We would have to revert to a robust and well-functioning house-church system and community-centric model which will keep the faith alive and strong. The problem of expanding the priesthood and delivering sacraments in such homes will have to be addressed by the traditional churches. Many modern Christians have lost touch with the Christianity offered by its founder, Jesus, but managed to embrace 'Churchianity'. For them going to church on Sunday was and is their religion. They would perhaps be the most hit with the lockdown—some will find other gods, or find their way back to their churches to continue their religious observances after the lockdown is lifted.

2. Territorial boundaries of the parish are fast disappearing. There is the issue of choice – as with burgeoning TV channels. With the Church going 'virtual' during the pandemic, territorial boundaries are fast disappearing. With no dearth of options available online for Communion services, sing-alongs and spiritual talks, the faithful can now easily surf channels till they find something that suits their interest and feeds their souls. A priest may have a 'captive audience' in church, but not so in cyberspace. Priests will have to work harder to make their sermons more profound, well-researched, reflective and contextual to the lives of the audience. While we acknowledge that the Church is not a building, many traditional churches sanctify their places of worship, and most of the faithful would find it difficult to exchange idea of the House of God for TV churches or house churches. The result could mean even less attendance in churches than ever before. Meanwhile most churches will remain clergy-centric and building-centred communities. This may require a change.

3. Income to parishes will dry up: With dwindling attendance, running and maintaining church buildings is going to get difficult, especially for the smaller churches. With electronic donations becoming the norm, people will no longer feel restrained to contribute only to the local parish but to the one that attracts them or gives them the spiritual sustenance they need.

4. E-Liturgies: Evangelical and Pentecostal Churches are better geared for TV evangelism. Not so the traditional [or mainline] churches. Although HH the Catholicos, the Head of the Orthodox Church in India gave permission to project liturgical services through electronic media—but only in these lockdown times—and the Catholic Church has been allowing it for the old and infirm, the long-term effects *after* lockdown can only be guessed. Perhaps we will have to use this lockdown to change our set ideas and worship in "spirit and truth" beyond temples and mountain (Jn 4:21-24), as Jesus suggested to the Samaritan woman.

5. False and misleading spirituality: With people turning to their hand-held devices to receive spiritual nourishment, the number of spiritual talks, Bible catechesis, retreats, etc., being offered online has ballooned exponentially. With the mushrooming of choices through the media comes the challenge – how does one distinguish and identify an authentic teaching based on the dogma and teaching of each individual church doctrine?

6. Online courses and retreats conducted by some churches and a few tech-savvy clergy have been around for some time, but that may soon become the norm. Will traditional conventions by top line speakers, courses and retreats find the same response, especially with the pressing demand on people's time in a chaotic urban landscape? They would more likely welcome those they could access at their convenience. Again, they will have more choice than they ever had before.

The above mentioned are only with regard to the institution of the Church; but understanding that there is an interconnectedness of things, don't we need to go beyond? Physically we keep getting faster, higher and stronger as the official Olympic motto taken from the Latin '*citius, altius, fortius*' in 1894 tells us. Mentally we have evolved in science and technology, and we try to conquer space—where we could find life. Yet it is difficult to understand why we humans have not been able to evolve spiritually. Over the last several centuries we have not evolved our methods of spiritual life. We are unable to go beyond the herd mentality of our forefathers, where family and tribe and clan were the basic building blocks of society.

We know today that the first human came from Africa and a common thread exists in the DNA of all humans, whatever be their country, colour, race or tribe. In spite of this we continue to divide ourselves into country, caste and tribe—highlighting the 'us versus them' binary—instead of seeing how we are interconnected. In spite of knowledge received from the latest scientific and technological advances, we are unable to see ourselves as a single species, humankind, who, instead of warring over territories and seas and trivial political and social issues, should band together to fight our common enemies like problems of poverty, water, pestilence, disease, climate change and the resultant environmental degradation, all of which do not favour any country or people or tribe over the other but could spell doom for all of us.

On Butterflies' Wings: Envisioning Common Faith, Common Worship

I will venture one step further. With a million tiny 'butterfly effects' that have been let loose on planet earth, and accepting more and more the interconnectedness of things, can this post-pandemic situation bring us to the knowledge and experience of a common faith in God, or faith in a common god? Can we envisage common worship centres, and common prayers? Emperor Akbar had such an idea though the *Dīn-i Ilāhī* (Persian: '*Religion of God*'), a syncretic religion propounded in 1582, intending to merge some of the elements of the religions of his empire, and thereby reconcile the differences that divided his subjects. It was denounced immediately as blasphemy then, and I am sure it will be the same today, by faith leaders, priests and theologians of every religion, who stand most to lose if such a preposterous idea becomes a reality. However, as we feel the effects of Covid-19, couldn't we give some thought to this as a basic rubric or as a prophetic possibility in the future?

This pandemic, initiated by a Wuhan butterfly, bat or pangolin, is likely to give rise to a lot more 'butterfly effects' over time across the globe, and, because of the interconnectedness of things, it might have repercussions that last longer, are possibly more lethal, and can be much more severe than we can currently predict. However, we can move forward with the comforting words of Jesus, "And, lo, I am with you always, even unto the end of the world" (Mt 28:20).

12

Groaning and Growing Anew: Post-Covid Church in India

Rajni Herman

Introduction: Afflicted but not Crushed

The unexpected and life threatening Covid-19 pandemic has thrown many of us off balance. The world of fear, unease and social distancing has gripped and rattled our anchoring. Sadly, none of us can say that we are and have been immune to the clutches of this virus. With the passage of time, the situation has taken a great toll on many—both physically and emotionally, and the Church has not been exempted from these hardships. Day by day the stark realities and unprecedented challenges—especially faced by our migrant labour force—have been seen all too clearly on television screens, social media platforms, newspapers and other sources. Those pathetic scenes have rattled many of us still further.

To flatten the Covid-19 curve of infection, the Government rightly announced various stringent prevention measures:

social distancing, lockdown of movement, prohibition of congregating as a Church as large religious gatherings were banned, etc. However, as a result, due to disruption of education, taking care of the elderly or children at home, struggles of Christian families with reduced or lost income and now the recent added cause of having to go back out and meet people, many within the Church are full of fear and anxiety. All this, coupled with the loneliness and isolation that many faced and are facing, brings to the forefront a potential mental health impact caused by the Covid-19 crisis. This impact needs much support from within the Church.

Seeking Christian Response to the Covid Crisis

So, the question arises: how does one even begin to deal with the constant array of complex emotional challenges and upheavals facing the congregants? What measures should the Church put in place to see to the mental wellness of her own, to those out there in our churches who are crying out like the psalmist: "Why are you cast down, oh my soul, why so disturbed within me?" How do we respond to the mental health impact that has been caused? The following five measures seem to offer possibilities for Christian commitment:

1. *Recall*: and deepen the certainty and reality of the infallible truths of the Bible, the promises, to show how God is omnipresent and therefore fully aware of every detail of our life at every moment and in every place. Through the lens of scripture, the Church needs to display the "holistic vision of who our Sovereign Lord is," the Great "I AM" who cares for us, who understands and knows the underlying fears and anxieties that assail us. God is

the answer to our despairing soul: "Give ear and come to me, hear me that your soul may live," says the Lord (Isa 55:3). He is the King and friend who promises: "And lo, I am with you always" (Mt 28:20). The post Covid-19 phase as a Church should be an era where amidst the threatening, stressful circumstances, we cultivate and strengthen, through the Word and prayer, faith and commitment to God and we draw people into a deeper, stronger, personal relationship with our Lord who has promised "to never leave nor forsake us" (Josh 1:5).

2. *Reassure*: that the Church is a 'safe place' for those struggling emotionally; they need to be welcomed and not shunned. We need to work with great sensitivity and present ourselves as a community that cares for its own, as well as for others. We must reassure the emotionally drained that they are not alone, that they are understood, seen, heard and loved. Their genuine concerns and deep-rooted fears need to be addressed with much empathy and love that flows out of the truth of "loving our neighbour as ourselves" and "looking out not for our own interests but the interests of others" (Phil 2:3).

3. *Regularity in staying connected*: There is security in staying connected. Those undergoing emotional upheavals need to stay connected with others. During the Covid crisis, members of churches have leveraged various tools and platforms and have made the best use of virtual meetings and social media to stay connected and to interact with one another. However, as the days unfold and gatherings are restored, there may be many among us who will not

feel comfortable to come back to a physical gathering. We need to continue to foster these relationships with great sensitivity to stay connected with these brothers and sisters. For us as believers in Christ, it is the love of Christ that compels us (2 Cor 5:14) to go out of our way to stay connected.

4. *Render service*: In our churches, the services of psychologists, counsellors, and lay leaders trained in counselling can prove essential during the post Covid stage, which will be challenging times for many members. The Church can organise personalised sessions with these counsellors and psychologists in order to provide the emotional support that some may require. For others, the sudden economic shutdown, downturn and job loss can trigger deep-seated anxiety, discouragement and depression. Various economic needs will arise within our churches to which we need to respond with much benevolence, generosity and kindness. It will be a call to continuously model love not just with words but with deeds and wallets too.

5. *Relationships*: As we walk through the challenging days that lie ahead, we need to make intentional efforts to delve deeper in our relationships with those confronted with fear and uncertainty. We will have to walk with them and encourage them. We will have to pray with them and for them. It is a call to increase in our servant-heartedness to them.

Conclusion: Growing towards A Glowing Hope

As we abide in Christ and walk by his Spirit through these challenging days, may we remember and encourage those struggling to hold on to the hope we have in Christ. Let us recollect what the apostle Paul wrote in Romans 8:22 -25: "We know that the whole creation has been groaning as in the pains of childbirth right up to the present time. Not only so, but we ourselves, who have the first fruits of the Spirit, groan inwardly as we wait eagerly for our adoption to sonship, the redemption of our bodies. For in this hope we were saved. But hope that is seen is no hope at all. Who hopes for what they already have? But if we hope for what we do not yet have, we wait for it patiently." Let us wait, then, our hearts full of hope in Him and Him alone.

13

Harbingers of Hope: Wedding Faith and Science in Covid Times

Samuel Richmond Saxena

Introduction: The Need for Dialogue between Science and Religion

As the world is battling with the Covid-19 pandemic, people from different walks of life are becoming more and more united as never seen before. Doctors, health professionals, scientists, economists, sociologists, theologians, artists, journalists, politicians, clinical psychologists, are responding to the impact of this deadly disease. This pandemic—which has affected the human race irrespective of caste, colour, region, race and nation—has brought all of us on the same platform to rethink some of the fundamental questions related to the meaning of life, human suffering, human destiny, etc. Science and religion are considered to be the most powerful institutions in this world. Unfortunately, the majority of those concerned and committed to these two domains do not see any commonality between them. It's vital now to bring them into dialogue to envision a new society.

Scientists and religionists are now puzzled and perturbed about Covid-19, which has posed a severe threat to society. Scientists are struggling to create a vaccine, while believers are trying to interpret scripture according to their belief systems. In an era when scientists boast about their achievements while religious heads claim receiving supernatural revelations from God, humanity still seems to lack something. People are desperately looking towards scientists and researchers for some vaccine, while religion is giving some hope to believers in these times of uncertainty.

Albert Einstein once commented, 'science without religion is lame, religion without science is blind.'[1] The biggest question for humanity is: How should we react towards the inventions of medical science as well as in the miraculous power of God at the same time? At this point, science (medicine and health care) and religion (faith) should together respond to address Covid-19 holistically.

Science in Quarantine

In September 2019, just before the outbreak of Covid-19, Jennifer Nuzzo, a senior scholar at the Johns Hopkins Center for Health Security and her colleagues published a WHO/ World Bank-commissioned report titled 'Preparedness for a High-Impact Respiratory Pathogen Pandemic.' In her interview with JSTOR Daily, Nuzzo said that the United States squandered the opportunity to prepare for the pandemic.[2] It is still uncertain how many scientists, medical doctors, politicians and religious leaders around the world took this publication seriously at that time.

Today, scientists, medical doctors, and others are working persistently to take things back to normal. Advancement in science and technology has taken us to that stage where physical science is getting ready to probe into the mysterious world of dark matter and dark energy, hopefully with the help of gravitational-wave technology; the invention of robots who act on our behalf, genome-edited human babies that are developed with HIV-resistant capabilities; space-travel in a few years of time may become an everyday affair.[3] But this tiny invisible virus has shocked and humbled scientists to rethink about the overall purpose of the natural world.

It is now important for medical science to work on the quality of the existing health care system to cope up with the next global health emergency by keeping other things aside. According to Francis Collins,[4] Covid-19 is ten times more infectious than influenza and it may take a year and a half to get the vaccine (in million doses) which is an ultimate solution.[5] Recently, the Department of Science and Technology in India has announced several special research projects to eradicate the virus, details of which are available on their website.

At this point science appears to be helpless. There are other major challenges that science cannot tackle alone. These are related to people's physical, spiritual, and mental status. Stress, anxiety, panic, depression and fear have gripped our people because of several factors: the loss of loved ones, economic crises, poverty, unemployment, separation from family and friends, self-isolation, social distancing, testing, the cry of the migrants, rapid increase in cases of domestic violence and so on. In such a situation, science which has quarantined itself from the people of faith has now to break the walls of isolation and work together with the community of believers who put their faith in God.

Faith in Quarantine

Covid-19 has not only pushed the educational system to go online but has also given opportunities for religions to worship online as a means of communicating with God and fellow believers. Through this method, Christians, Jews and Muslims were bound to celebrate Easter, Passover and Eid ul Fitr, respectively, during the lockdown period. Across the globe, people are witnessing online weddings, funerals and other religious activities. There is a paradigm shift from conventional theological education to an online system that may open up new opportunities and several challenges. Initially, for some religious heads, it was a nightmare to close down their religious places. In India, as per the health ministry, thirty percent of the coronavirus was spread because of those who returned from a large gathering at the Markaz (Centre), the headquarters of the Tablighi Jamat, a conservative Islamic organisation, New Delhi.[6] The chief of Tablighi Jamaat Markaz, Maulana Saad has blamed the sins of humankind for the novel corona virus. The matter is still under investigation.[7]

During this period, we have often come across many preachers who are quoting from the Book of Deuteronomy 28:20-22 which states that the Lord attacks people with plagues, curses, confusions, fever and inflammations and 2 Chronicles 7:13,14 where it is stated that [God] will "command the locust to devour the land or send pestilence among my people, if my people who are called by my name humble themselves, pray, seek my face, and turn from their wicked ways, then I will hear from heaven, and will forgive their sin and heal their land." Some religious preachers falsely quote the incidence of corona virus as a God-perpetrated penalty on humans because of their wickedness. Apart from the modern medicinal approach, traditional therapeutic practices from China, India and Africa—well-rooted in culture and indigenous religion—are also trying to stand as alternative medicine during this pandemic. But all these need to be well researched before used; or else we will face greater problems.

Harmony between Science and Religion: Harbingers of Hope
Though science and religion may mutually benefit from each other, there are still some contradictions which remain between the two. Is Covid-19 a spiritual disease as a result of punishment from God as claimed by the majority of religious leaders? Or it is a pathogenic disease that should be left for only science and medics to manage?[8] At this juncture, the blend of these two powerful influences is required to give a solution. Humility among scientists and religious leaders should be the foremost priority before they interact. Pope John Paul II once wrote to Fr George Coyne, S.J., the former director of the Vatican Observatory, that: "Science can purify religion from error and superstition; religion can purify science from idolatry and false absolutes. Each can draw the other into a wider world, a world in which both can flourish."

Ian Barbour, the famous physicist and theologian, once expressed that life of all creatures on this planet is so interconnected to each other that it should be experienced in wholeness rather than by looking into separate compartments.[9] We don't know how many pandemics the world is going to face in the future. We can only pray that it may not happen; but if it does, we should all come together and trust in the living God who is almighty and grants wisdom to the people who seek His direction.

King Solomon who is considered to be the wisest person on the earth wrote, "It is the glory of God to conceal things, but the glory of kings is to search things out" (Prov 25:2). It is a matter of trust. Jesus said "If you have faith as small as a mustard seed, you can say to this mountain, 'Move from here to there,' and it will move. Nothing will be impossible for you" (Mt 17:20). We have a hope to give to the world because through the power of God, all of creation receives redemption, healing and restoration. We are called to take care of God's creation as responsible and good stewards. Above all, our mission is to share the message of peace, harmony and reconciliation to those who are suffering.

Endnotes

[1] Einstein: Science and Religion in http://einsteinandreligion.com/scienceandreligion2.html

[2] 'Rigorous testing key to fight Covid-19: Johns Hopkins epidemiologist' in https:/ www.outlookindia.com/newsscroll rigorous-testing-key-to-fight-covid19-johns-hopkins-epidemiologist/1797099 09 April 2020.

[3] Job Kozhamthadam, 'Corona Cornering Humans: Another Humbling Experience of Science' in https://www.issr.org.uk/blog/april-2020-blog-post-science-religion-coronavirus/

[4] Dr Francis Collins is a physician and geneticist known for spearheading the Human Genome Project and for his landmark discoveries of disease genes. Presently he is the director of the National Institutes of Health, US

[5] Responding to the Coronavirus with Faith and Common Sense – Dr. Francis Collins in https://www.youtube.com/watch?v=OG39Cy1FBq4

[6] 'Nearly 30% coronavirus cases across India linked to Nizamuddin Markaz: Health Ministry' https://economictimes.indiatimes.com/news/politics-and-nation/nearly-30-coronavirus-cases-across-india-linked-to-nizamuddin-markaz-health-ministry/videoshow/75221783.cms?from=mdr

[7] 'Allah is angry: Tablighi Jamaat Markaz chief blames sins of mankind for coronavirus' https://www.indiatoday.in/india/story/allah-is-angry-tablighi-jamaat-markaz-chief-blames-sins-of-mankind-for-coronavirus-1662612-2020-04-02

[8] Bernard Alwala, 'What Has Science to Do with Religion? A Looming Challenge of Traditional and Religious Practices on Curbing the Spread of Covid-19 Pandemic in Kenya' in *East African Journal of Traditions, Culture and Religion* vol. 2, issue 1, 2020, p.31.

[9] Alister E. McGrath, *Science & Religion: A New Introduction* (Oxford: Blackwell Publishers, 2010), p.47.

14

Corona Call to Heal Our Sick Mother Earth

Chilkuri Vasantha Rao

Introduction: Humankind Moulded out of Our Mother Earth

The very word 'mother earth' indicates our origins in the earth. This is because we are drawn out from the body and the elements of the earth. The Hebrew word for earth is *Adamah* which is a feminine noun just as our biological mother is a female. Hence, we realize that our existence is tied up with the earth and that human being was called Adam, which means the one derived out of *Adamah*: the earth. "…Lord God formed man (*Adam*) from the dust of the earth (*Adamah*)…" (Gen 2:7). The human being in the Hebrew connotation is actually called an 'earthling', we are all 'earthlings' formed out of the 'earth'. So then, *Adam* is the child, and *Adamah*, the earth, is the mother.

When created by God, this mother earth was hale and healthy: "God called the dry land earth …. And God saw that it was good" (Gen 1:10). The earth was very good (Gen 1:31) in its symbiotic relationship with the rest of the created order. Human children have particularly become defiant and turned violent against the mother earth making her totally sick with their sickening lifestyle. If we measure the temperature of the sick mother earth it indicates that she is suffering from global warming. The causes for this sickness are: we have chocked the earth with our air pollution, suffocated her with our water pollutants, terrified her with our bombardments, shamed her with deforestation, plundered her wealth with our greed, stripped her of her garment—the ozone layer, and left her naked gasping on a pyre. We have made our mother earth weak, sick and vulnerable!

Mother Earth Suffers at the Hands of Her Children

When a mother suffers, her whole family suffers. The word of God indicates how humans have treated mother earth. "…. Before them the land is like the garden of Eden, but after them a desolate wilderness…." (Joel 2:3). When the earth's life is at stake then all life dependent upon the earth is also at risk. The Bible informs us of this repercussion: "Wail, O cypress, for the cedar has fallen, for the glorious trees are ruined! Wail, oaks of Bashan, for the thick forest has been felled! Hark, the wail of the shepherds, for their glory is despoiled. Hark, the roar of the lions, for the jungle of the Jordan is laid waste! (Zech 11:2-3). A dirge is heard everywhere. It is not only the wailing for the trees, humans and animals but also of the earth. "Therefore, the land mourns, and all who live in it languish" (Hos 4:3).

Covid-19 corona virus is a grave example how humanity has not set its priorities right and has played into the hands of death forces. In the very creation God has kept certain things separate; for instance, separated light from the darkness (Gen 1:4), separated waters (Gen 1:7), separated the day from the night (Gen 1:14). And so, God has separated life and death, and called us to choose life (Deut 30:19). But with Covid-19, instead of choosing life, we have invited death into our midst This pandemic has overcome humanity. We have given death the upper hand.

World governments have regulated lockdowns, medical staff have risked their lives, police have engaged themselves in the implementation of the lockdown, local municipal bodies have seen to the sanitisation. Umpteen numbers of NGOs and Churches have plunged into action in caring for the poor and the stranded migrant workers. Lockdown phases are now being reversed with unlocking plans. But all is not okay. What is the role of the Church in the post Covid scenario? A theological understanding and a biblical direction would guide us into the future.

A Biblical Vision and Dream

Earth is a living organism; we call it mother earth. When we talk of the earth, we acknowledge the earth and its fullness thereof (Ps 24:1). Human beings are but a part of that fullness, not the entire fullness. What then are the implications for the Church, its ministry and mission?

Being in a profound contemplative mood, one night I had a dream, wherein a person introduced to me a priest/pastor, who was wearing a cassock and a sash with a cross hanging from around the neck, saying: "S/he is the Director of Earth

Relations." This was a new concept. We are aware of 'Directors of Ecumenical Relations', 'Directors of International Relations', and 'Public Relations Officers'. If the priest is analogous to the Church, then, how does the Church assume responsibility for the healing of our sick mother earth?

How would we envisage a priest being the Director of the Earth Relations? A priest is normally called as 'the parish priest/pastor'. This then compels us to reflect on the word 'parish'. A parish is a geographical area served by a priest/pastor. The Greek root word for 'parish' is from "an alteration of Late Greek *paroikia* 'a diocese or *parish*', from *paroikos* 'a sojourner'…, in classical Greek, 'neighbour', from *para* - near … + *oikos* - 'house.'"[1] The "use of *paroikos* in the ancient world … both the adjective and the substantive is representative: adj.: 'dwelling beside or near, neighbouring'; subst.: 'neighbour, sojourner in another's house'; generally, 'aliens, stranger.'"[2] Both the words *paroikia* and *paroikos* indicate a larger scope of a parish.

Paroikia 'a parish' is not to be understood as comprising only of the subscribed members of the congregation, but a parish comprises of *paroikos* that are living in that geographical limits. All who are *para* 'near' the *oikos* 'house', i.e., all the neighbours that are in the parish's geographical boundaries. Who are those neighbours? The law "love your neighbour as yourself" is found in Leviticus 19:18. Verse 19 indicates that those neighbours are the: (a) animals, (b) plants, (c) materials, and then human beings are mentioned in verse 20. In other words, a parish comprises of all neighbours of the neighbourhood in the geographical area, which is under the care of a priest or pastor.

A priest/pastor, in the real sense of the word, is indeed the Director of Earth Relations. S/he is not only to care for the human members of the Church but also every inhabitant of the created order in the priest's geographical precincts. The pastor is to care for the *jameen* (earth), *jal* (water), *jungle* (forest) *jeevan* (all life, i.e., all living beings). This needs to be the ideal, holistic, and comprehensive approach to the pastoral ministry that will ensure the healing of the weakened and sick mother earth.

Conclusion: Church Called to Build the *Kin-dom* of God for Fuller Life

In the post Covid-19 context, the Church is to assume this new inclusive ministry to the entire Life and Life forms and Life systems. A priest/pastor would broaden the scope of his/her ministry to all else. A parish would take into account all the inhabitants in its boundaries. Jesus was good in Earth Relations; he mentioned the birds, grass, flowers, water, animals, sky, earth, air, fields and other beings in his teachings. Jesus was holistic and inclusive in his mission of establishing the Kin-dom-of-God, where the earth and all the inhabitants of and earth are the kith and kin, today gasping for breath, awaiting a speedy recovery and a new fullness of Life.

Endnotes

[1] https://www.britannica.com/topic/history-of-Europe/The-structure-of-ecclesiastical-and-devotional-life#ref994474 accessed on June 2, 2020.

[2] John H. Elliott, *A Home for The Homeless: A Sociological Exegesis of I Peter, Its Situation and Strategy*, Philadelphia, Fortress Press, 1981, p.24.

Contributors

Rev. Asir Ebenezer is an ordained minister of the CSI Diocese of Madras, presently serving as the General Secretary of the National Council of Churches in India. Since 1991, Asir has been involved in facilitating churches to socio-political engagement in the world. He continues to serve the Indian, regional and global ecumenical movement in various capacities.

Prof. Rev. Dr Chilkuri Vasantha Rao is a Presbyter of the CSI Medak Diocese, currently the Principal of the United Theological College, Bengaluru. He is a dedicated Pastor, theological educator and an able administrator committed to serve the Indian Church. He is a lyricist, composer, singer and ballad dancer, with wide outreach on the internet..

Prof. Dr Felix Wilfred is currently Founder-Director, Asian Centre for Cross-Cultural Studies, Chennai. Earlier he was the Head of the Department of Christian Studies, and Chairman of the School of Philosophy and Religious Thought, University of Madras. He was the first holder of the Chair of Indian Studies, Trinity College, Dublin. As a visiting professor, he has taught in different universities in Asia, the USA and

Europe. He edited *The Oxford Handbook of Christianity* in Asia. Several of his books were published by ISPCK, Delhi.

Prof. Dr Francis Gonsalves is a Jesuit professor and journalist. He has a Licentiate from the Gregorian University, Rome, and a Doctorate from the University of Madras. He was Principal of the Vidyajyoti College, Delhi, and is currently Dean of Theology at the Jnana-Deepa Vidyapeeth, Pune. He has also lectured abroad. He has authored seven books, edited eight others, publishes scholarly articles and writes fortnightly for *The Asian Age* and *The Deccan Chronicle* national dailies. His interests include interfaith dialogue, interdisciplinary approaches to theology and social-justice issues.

Rev. Hemalatha John is an ordained presbyter in-charge, presently ministering in the Church South India-Karnataka Central diocese. She completed her Bachelor of Divinity from Serampore University, India and Masters in Intercultural Theology from Goettingen University, Germany. In addition, she is a Director of Ecology and Environmental Concerns in Karnataka Central Diocese and involved in various Ecumenical and Ecclesial concerns.

Rev. Dr Packiam T. Samuel is an ordained priest from the Church of South India. He is presently the Director of Henry Martyn Institute, Hyderabad. He is an avid proponent of interfaith relations. He teaches Religions at the Henry Martyn Institute and Advanced Institute for Research on Religion and Culture (a federated programme of Andhra Christian Theological Studies, Calvin Institute of Theology and Henry Martyn Institute—affiliated to the Senate of Serampore College [University]).

Fr Philip Kuruvilla is an ordained minister in the Indian Orthodox Church. He holds a Masters of Theology from Oxford University and another in Social Work from Nagpur RTM University. He is an author and editor of several books, and he has produced few documentary video films. He was the Dean of the Orthodox Seminary in Nagpur. Subsequently he has been working with the National Council of Churches in India and the Christian Conference of Asia in the field of Human Rights, HIV & AIDS, and Sexual Minority Issues. Now retired in Bengaluru with his wife, he has started an NGO called *"The Untouchables"*.

Dr Rajni Herman is a pastors wife and a medical doctor, and a mother of two teenage girls. She resides in Delhi. She is the Project Director of Shalom Delhi - A Palliative care unit of Emmanuel Hospital Association.

Dr Rini Ralte is a Professor and Chairperson of the Department of Women's Studies at the United Theological College, Bangalore. The department of Women's Studies celebrated their Silver Jubilee and celebrated in March 7, 2020. Dr Ralte hails from Mizoram and belongs to the Presbyterian Church of Mizoram, and a local Church Elder at Bangalore Presbyterian Church. She is Tribal Ecofeminist Theologian and Activist of Women's Rights.

Rev. Samuel Richmond Saxena (Ph.D., Sam Higginbottom University) is University Chaplain and Head of the Department of Advanced Theological Studies, Faculty of Theology, Sam Higginbottom University of Agriculture, Technology and Sciences, Prayagraj, India. A member of the World Evangelical

Alliance Theological Commission, he is the author of *Contemporary Issues in Science and Theology* (2018). He is also the Chaplain (UP & UK Region) of the Christian Medical Association of India, New Delhi.

Dr Shalini Mulackal is a Presentation Sister and a Professor of systematic theology at Vidyajyoti College of Theology, Delhi. She is also a visiting professor to a number of other Seminaries, and theological institutes. She is a member of the Indian Theological Association (ITA) and has been its first woman President. She is also a member of the Indian Women Theologians Forum (IWTF), Ecclesia of Women of Asia (EWA) and Indian Christian Women's Movement (ICWM). She has published many articles and contributed essays to many books with special emphasis on women empowerment.

Rev. Dr Sunil Caleb did his B.D. from United Theological College, Bengaluru. He was a deacon and presbyter in the Diocese of Amritsar, CNI, for 5 years. He did his Ph.D. in Christian Ethics from the University of Kent at Canterbury, England. He joined Bishop's College and later became Principal of the College in 2008.

Rev. Dr Vincent Rajkumar is an ordained minister of the Church of South India. Currently he is serving as the Director of Christian Institute for the Study of Religion and Society (CISRS), Bangalore.

Rev. Vinod Victor is a Presbyter of the South Kerala Diocese of the Church of South India and is Chairperson of Asia CMS. He served as the Synod Youth Secretary of the Church of South India and as Coordinator of the South Asia Ecumenical

Partnership Programme (SAEPP) an initiative of the WCC and CCA. He has also served parishes in India and Australia. He now ministers to the Holy Trinity CSI Church in Trivandrum.

www.ingramcontent.com/pod-product-compliance
Lightning Source LLC
LaVergne TN
LVHW040219180726
843492LV00011B/569